Artem Chekh

Absolute Zero

ABSOLUTE ZERO

by Artem Chekh

Translated from the Ukrainian
by Olena Jennings and Oksana Lutsyshyna

Proofreading by Michael Wharton

Book cover and layout interior created by Max Mendor

Publishers Maxim Hodak & Max Mendor

© 2020, Artem Chekh

© 2020, Olena Jennings and Oksana Lutsyshyna

© 2020, Glagoslav Publications

www.glagoslav.com

ISBN: 978-1-91289-468-0

A catalogue record for this book is available from the British Library.

Artem Chekh

Absolute Zero

Translated from the Ukrainian
by Olena Jennings and Oksana Lutsyshyna

GLAGOSLAV PUBLICATIONS

Contents

PART I
Absolute Zero

New Dreams

The bus bearing the slogan sign "Everybody Dance!" painted across its side looked like it was ferrying passengers to a spa rather than a boot camp. There were forty-one drafted men and two accompanying officers. We were en route to the Rivne basic training camp.

When the city high-rises ended and the forest began, I almost cried. I was sentimental, moved by the anticipation of a new life. I was puzzled by my new role, excited by the unknown. I was filled with something like a desire to put on my uniform as soon as possible, to walk around in camouflage, just like all those I watched during this last year with mixed feelings of admiration and guilt, though I knew I would be drafted. If not in January, then in April. You always have a gut feeling about such things. I even quit my job. Wanted to finish writing a book. Ran out of time.

The bus stopped and men moved toward the door. Somebody elbowed me. Instead of an "excuse me," he uttered an expletive.

"The toilets are behind the gas station," one of the officers politely informed us. "Just please no hooch, guys."

"No hooch," we agreed.

Some men had already purchased alcohol the day before, and it was now carefully packed away or poured into plastic lemonade bottles.

We were standing around smoking. One short guy recounted, "For twenty years now I've been having a recurring dream that I was drafted into the army. I tell these people that I've already completed my draft time, and they say, 'Hell no, you're gonna serve.' And in that dream I'm on the bus, at a train station, my boots too tight. Since the war in Donbas started, I dream about this every night. And sure thing, the draft card came, and now I'm on my way. Just like in my dream."

The others nodded, agreeing, sighing, and one after another shared stories and fables. They recalled Soviet mercenaries in Libya and Egypt in

THE **BIG** GIVE

Give online at **foundationforbcpl.org/librarybiggive** or use the form below.

☐ Yes, I want to support the Foundation!

☐ $75   ☐ $150   ☐ $250   ☐ $500   ☐ $1,000   ☐ $ _____

_____
Name

_____
Address

_____
City/State/Zip

_____
Phone   Email

How you wish your name(s) to appear on donor recognition

☐ I wish this gift to remain anonymous.   ☐ I do not want any physical incentives.

PAYMENT OPTIONS:

☐ Online at **foundationforbcpl.org.**

☐ Cash or check is enclosed
   (*checks payable to Foundation for Baltimore County Public Library*).

☐ VISA   ☐ MasterCard   ☐ AmEx   ☐ Discover

_____
Card Number

_____
Exp. Date

_____
Name on Card

☐ I would like more information about supporting the library with a planned
   gift to the Foundation (*such as in your will or naming the Foundation as a
   retirement plan beneficiary*).

Return form to: Foundation for Baltimore County Public Library,
              Attn: Julie Saxenmeyer, 320 York Road, Towson, MD 21204

foundationforbcpl.org/librarybiggive

THE BIG GIVE

Connect with Your Library

Make a BIG impact
May 18

This May, Foundation for Baltimore County Public Library needs you to be a part of something **BIG**. One **BIG** day to **EXPLORE** how we can make a difference, to **LEARN** something new, to **CREATE** fresh opportunities and to **CONNECT** the community.

THE BIG GIVE, the Foundation's official day of giving, is coming! Join us on Wednesday, May 18 in a show of support for your local library. There will be events at branches around the county, a Facebook Live event and giveaways, all culminating in a free sunset concert featuring Bad w/ Names on the rooftop of the Towson Branch garage from 6 p.m.-8 p.m. Watch the Foundation's social media for more info coming this month.

Donate $75 or more to automatically become an All In Crowd member and receive a BIG mug!

foundationforbcpl.org/librarybiggive

1976, Afghanistan in 1989, and Yugoslavia in 1994. A volunteer who spent twenty-six years as an ambulance driver kept urging everyone to give up alcohol, repeating the officer's words.

We got back on the bus and started off again. Tired from excitement, everybody was whispering nervously, despondently watching the landscape through the windows. Everybody was drinking.

I chowed down on some sandwiches: cheap white bread with processed cheese. I was thinking, should I offer some to anyone else? Do I look like a scrooge? Or is it too soon? Maybe later when we get to know each other better?

I was looking at those who were drinking something resembling cognac from plastic bottles. They didn't share either. They were just drinking their own stuff. So I relaxed. I thought about my wife, only yesterday standing with me in front of the Selective Service office. She was lost in thought, her life about to change, starting a new chapter without me, the cold nights, the anxious mornings. How long would it be before we saw each other again? A month? A year? Two? Forever?

Standing there with her I thought, for the first time, that I was living somebody else's life. And from then on, I would have somebody else's dreams. And occupy somebody else's place, to become a hero, or a coward. Or die.

One way or another, each of us would have new dreams.

The Hour of Freedom Fighters

Having passed the admin building and arriving at the tent city, the first thing I see is sand and hair. Instead of dirt it is all sand, partly turned into dust. And hair. Long and short, black, red, gray strands cover the ground as if forming a shag rug. The evening breeze blows the hair, and it flies over the tents like pollen from a poplar tree. Near the generators the men sit on stools. Their skin is very tanned. Their heads are being shaved by other shaved men with soft stomachs and scars all over their bodies from old surgeries.

I walk together with the dozen Kyivites who had been summoned with me to the Selective Service office, timidly between the tents, catching curious glances thrown at us by the locals.

"Guys, where are you from?" we hear them ask. "Kyiv," we answer. "Capital boys! Haha!" This reminds me slightly of classic scenes from movies where the hero ends up in prison and walks through the prison block to his own cell.

Our uniforms are too new, our boots too shiny, our skin still retains the paleness of winter, we have too many expensive cigarettes in our pockets, and on our heads are the remnants of stylish haircuts.

We immediately line up in formation. Along the ranks of the fourth platoon, a lieutenant with a pot belly slowly walks by. He is dressed in a new British uniform with a camouflage pattern. He insults the soldiers, chain smokes and openly mocks the troops. Approximately one hundred of the drafted men in my company look like inmates. Some immediately react to the lieutenant's jokes and laugh, revealing their black, toothless mouths. The scent of sweat and alcohol emanates from their skin.

Over the tents new and old ragged flags fly: yellow and blue, black and red, the colors of independence. Beyond the tent city, heaps of trash burn slowly. It reeks of latrines. Oh God, I think, how did I end up here? Who are all these people and where are all the brave and athletic young men from the ads? Where are all the lawyers, designers, journalists and salesmen? Where are those who sold their Rolls Royce for an opportunity at the front? What kind of a guerrilla unit is this, what kind of anarchy? How can I press Control Z and return to the clean streets of the capital, and my spotless office?

I am standing in my new, not-yet-faded uniform, and near my feet is a Polish backpack distributed to us along with the uniform, and the red Deuter backpack. My palms are sweaty, and from this very moment I realize that there is no turning back. Together with the cavalry, on top of a machine gun cart, with a bayonet in one hand and an early twentieth-century semi-automatic rifle in the other, there is only drowning in blood, following orders, shooting, and somehow, along the lines, not going mad from the suffocating Hour of Freedom Fighters. This is how it is: initiation, hair-cutting ritual, baptism with dirt and shit.

"Get used to it," says Lyosha, who came here with me. But unlike me, he has experience in the army. He is an expert in local customs and habits.

Twilight sets in. Mosquitos buzz over the tent city. The company leaders take us on an excursion to a local bathroom. It is long, thirty meters or so, covered with boards that were removed, most likely, from some shed. Near the walls, there are two narrow trenches. They are filled with excrement, white chloride powder, and blood. It seems that hemorrhoids are the most common disease here.

For a second, I imagine how tomorrow morning I'll be doing my business sitting butt to butt with others. I try to banish this image by thinking about what will happen to me in a month or two – with a short haircut, suntanned, with flaky skin on my face and my hands dirty from cheap machine oil. I will be sitting on a stool near a tent, watching the new arrivals. I might even be spitting from time to time. My new uniform will fade into a light ochre color, my combat boots will be permanently gray from dust, my feet will become calloused. Ahead of me there will be new trials, my regiment called to active duty, probably to war. I may even be maimed or killed... but at this point I am so new, I smell of fresh sweat and Givenchy after-shave. I am wounded by these images and struck by a premonition of the inevitable.

Ah yes, and my freedom-fighting commander stands over there, that fat asshole in the British uniform.

One Day in the Life

The most poignant dreams come right before sunrise. Usually it is something from civilian life – my wife, my son, the people from my past, college years, high school. These visions leave me uneasy and disturbed, because after you wake up you realize that you've already stopped belonging to yourself. "Where am I? Why me?" you ask for the umpteenth time, crawling out of your sleeping bag. "And what will this new day bring me?"

These first thirty minutes of the new day are not kind to you, as the demons of doubt and fear unleash themselves upon you while you are still drowsy. But as soon as I have breakfast and endure the humiliating routine of morning formation, the fog in my head dissipates, and everything settles. Fears dissolve, dreams are forgotten, and I don't feel the murky hatred toward my commander as I did in my dream. He is also less irritated with us.

We go to the training fields. At 8:00 a.m. the sun already burns our necks and noses. Our boots kick up a thick wall of white dust. It's hard to breathe. From time to time, we start running. But we keep talking anyway. What about? We talk about our previous jobs, past experiences, the tragedies we lived through, the boundaries crossed, and, of course, about weapons and their characteristics. Though truth be told, weapons, with abbreviations instead of names, hardly speak to me. And how could they, if I was one of those few at school who always skipped the chapters about war in Tolstoy's *War and Peace*?

They teach us to shoot. Some of the experienced men say that they teach us all wrong, that at the front nobody shoots this way. They teach us to crawl and to dig trenches. And they teach us to run, a lot, as if all we'll be doing is running away from death, or chasing it. All this training is reinforced by extreme attitudes from the instructors: from maniacal rigor with paperwork, reports, and our signatures in each column to a laissez-faire attitude about safety. We either stand in lines for hours to receive thirty bullets and sign tens of documents or we are given wooden crates of RPGs and do not keep track of what we blow up.

Running and crawling are, at least, simple. Here you have only your legs and feet, the wind at your back, and your heart. It is good if your heart is healthy. For some, running turns into a macabre exercise with the inevitable finish of falling to the ground and swallowing dry sand. Water is poured on them. They are transported to a field hospital, and heart meds are placed into their parched mouths. In such cases the instructor yells:

"These are The Two Hundred! – this is military slang for dead. – They are the fuckin' dead! To hell with them! Let's run, boys!"

And run we do. I am thinking about The Two Hundred. Well, at least judging from their faces and their ages, they have been Two Hundred for a while now. They just don't know it yet.

We return to the camp. We have lunch, we clean our weapons. At 4:00 P.M., there is formation and more training, till dark. Sometimes the instructors are too lazy to take us to the field, so we sit in tents. We melt from the heat, wait for supper, stand in line at the commissary where we can buy everything we need, except alcohol.

I try to focus on reading. But from the very first week in this camp I realized that I'd have to forget about reading for the time being. I just can't – the radio is too loud, the heat too strong, and the new experience and conditions are emotionally more gripping than any texts.

At night I crawl into my sleeping bag. The nights here are cold, like on the prairie. I cover myself with a blanket. Somebody got a television from somewhere, and now it competes with the radio. Somebody starts frying potatoes at midnight. From outside I hear the angry dealings of scouts and artillery men. The fifty-watt bulb that hangs lonely from the ceiling blinds me as if we're being interrogated in prison. I cover my head with my jacket.

I fall asleep. Through the fog and sweet nightmare, I struggle to figure out what I'm doing here. Come on, man (I'm angry with myself). You wanted it so much! You really wanted to play this game – the comic Major Payne, or some other war hero! You wanted training and drills until you fell over, fighting till victory, and a return from war as a decorated veteran! You wanted to become one of them! You wanted to get a taste of real patriotism! So suck it up. Get used to it! Or let yourself go to hell.

Passions over a Leave

The newly drafted can be divided into those who would love to leave at least for a day and those who are overall satisfied with an uninterrupted stay at the training field. The first kind mostly consists of family men and drunks whom they call avatars. Beyond the training field is regular civilian life which they have already grown unaccustomed to like to an old lover, but memory makes them excited, and they smile nervously hearing the word "LEAVE."

For two days, one day, or a few hours. In my regiment, there is a man who spent four hours at home. The other ten he was on the road. But he did manage to see his wife and kids, as well as drink some milk and eat homemade *kotlety*.

For some, even to go to Rivne, the closest town around here, is a luxury. The town has cafés, ATM machines, and supermarkets. Also, in the town one can have a drink. Not the local hooch, which can send you to the hospital, but decent, and, most importantly, safely manufactured vodka. And then it feels like a special kind of chic to ride in a *marshrutka*, a crowded minibus that is the only means of transportation in some areas of the city, while half-drunk, wearing a uniform, ignoring the disgusted looks that the passengers throw at you.

Because of avatars, the commanders are not particularly willing to let the more responsible soldiers into town. Sometimes, though, the commanders have no good reason. – *No.* – *Why?* – *Because I said so.*

But sometimes it is the other way around: the officer is in a good mood, so he lets half the platoon have a leave, some for a day, some for three days, and some for three hours.

The city terrifies, fascinates, and excites the soldiers who are not used to it. Long-forgotten feelings surface, something nostalgic, foggy, from childhood. And there you are, a child, after spending three weeks at summer camp situated between a narrow river and newly planted pines, returning home, walking through the town, recognizing and recalling it, gazing at the buildings that were most significant to you... People wearing civilian clothes surprise you the most. "You exist? Thank you, I like looking at you." In a coffee shop you go to the bathroom and see yourself in the mirror for pretty much the first time that week. "Hey man, is it really you? You've changed." On the streets, you break the habit of spitting onto the ground or blowing your nose through one nostril. You step back gasping when bicycles go by and you watch out when crossing the street. It takes so little: a smiling waitress wearing plastic earrings, two Americanos, a pastry called "Tenderness," fifteen minutes in a bookstore, half an hour in a park, two pounds of strawberries, the restless sounds of the city. All of this can be found in Rivne. This time around I was not allowed to spend my leave in my hometown.

They are afraid to let us go on leave. The natural instinct would be not to return. They are afraid that you will stab or shoot somebody on your way home. Or rape. Or you'll eat somebody's chihuahua. Or you'll shit under a monument to a revered artist. Or you'll arrive drunk. Or you won't arrive at all, just like Vovchyk from Verkhovyna. They say he had joined as a volunteer. The joke is that he climbed down the mountains to buy matches and was grabbed by recruiters. He does not even have state-issued ID, just an ID card from his forestry. Vovchyk served well, never malingered, never accepted an invitation to drink. And then he asked for a leave for four days, to commemorate forty days of the passing of his father, an important occasion for a religious person. And he never came back: he's had it with the military service. The case was handed over to the prosecutor's office.

This meant problems for the commanders, presumption of guilt for the soldiers, and, possibly, a five-year jail term for Vovchyk.

Or there is another one, a new guy from Luhansk. He seemed pleasant and calm, and even played sports. He asked for a leave to go to the town and was late coming back, claiming he got lost. He returned drunk, with an unfinished vodka bottle and a beer in his backpack. He was standing in front of the platoon and pitifully apologizing, saying that all this was caused by his childhood trauma, babbling something about his dad and the fresh breath of freedom. One more soldier managed to steal deodorant from a supermarket, and was brought back by the police... The desire to break away from the army at least for a few hours makes many soldiers resort to all kinds of cunning behaviors, such as scheming, lying, flattering, and offering bribes. One commander, for example, accepts only gadgets and appliances.

A little bit of time outside of the training field gives you strength, lets you feel like a civilian, and that means free. The army is trying to make you get used to a routine and discipline, but at first, this is a lost cause. In a month, one cannot achieve this; there is no way to break one's will or to compensate for its absence. Eventually the soldiers do grow accustomed, of course. They make peace with the circumstances, become integrated into the system, become its part, though not an inherent part, and sometimes even redundant. They sit on the benches near their tent, smoke, tell jokes, anxiously think about the eastern front, hope to return home, and despair about death. But not today, for sure, not today.

Dmytryk

Dmytryk, or Dima, is about forty. His family awaits his return to the Chernivtsi region. He calls his wife every day. Asks her to say hello and sends some "kissies" to his children, in a voice unfitting for a grown man.

His youngest son is five. Dima also says hello to him. At times he talks to his daughter. His intonation ranges from tenderness and humor to the seriousness of mentoring. I have been thinking for the last three weeks that he is the kind of a guy I could be friends with. Real friends. From time to time he gives me chocolates. He helps with the weapons or with simple everyday life advice: how to tie boots more efficiently, where to get wood to repair the bunks, or with what to wash an inflamed eye (for some reason I got conjunctivitis). I am, of course, grateful for his care, I tell him earnestly about my family, about the people I met in life, about sadness, pain, truth, and happiness. He listens attentively and believes every word I say.

Every morning Dima gets up at 5 and runs several kilometers around pine grove. He runs in black boots. He taught me how to soften them for such purposes. "They will be soft like the boots of Yosiph Vissarionovich," he explained. He means Stalin. But after Dima saw my summer boots, which are at least three times lighter than the ones we were given, the boots that I bought with my own money, he only shrugged and told me I would be fine.

After his run, Dima sits down on a stool near the tent, polishes his boots and lights a cigarette. He does not smoke much: no more than ten cigarettes a day, but he does so with gusto, enjoying every drag. He does not eat much either. Perhaps, for his five feet, two inch frame it is enough. But Dima always has chocolates or rolls in his pockets, and he gives those to the guys he is friendly with.

It's easy to talk to him. He could be my father (though he is nothing like my father). Or, maybe, more like an older brother (I don't have one). Dima from Chernivtsi. Chernivtsi's Dima.

Sometimes I jokingly call him Dmytryk, a diminutive of Dmytro. He laughs. It'll be easy for him to be at war. Technically, the war begins for him today. The thirtieth brigade is dispatched somewhere towards the town of Popasna. They say there is unrest there. But Dima will manage. And return to his wife and children for sure. And never again will he have to say hello to them over long distance, since from then on he will be living with them on the same street in his native village. This is how people often live in villages.

My father and grandfather, may God grant them long lives, live next to one another, in houses next door, Dima says. And everybody on the three streets has the same last name.

Many wanted to be part of the thirtieth brigade. Everyone has heard about it. A military community, a well-adjusted organism, suffers many losses but boasts even more heroic deeds. But from the whole scouting platoon only Dima was chosen. And there he is, collecting his things into the backpack. He gives me his bag of toffee, stoically thanks me for my decency, wishes me good aim and a clear head, promises to call, puts his backpack over his shoulders, and he takes his black duffel bag into his right hand. Then, not even bending in the slightest beneath the weight, he exits the tent. That's it. I am left alone with the thirty others. The lieutenant comes and says that in two days we will all be given assignments, even those of us who are avatars or imbeciles. "Even homosexuals," he adds for some reason. These last words suddenly create quite a stir in the tent. All kinds of dirty jokes follow. We're waiting. In an hour, we have to go to the evening shooting exercises. I forgot that I've already cleaned my weapon today, and start to take it apart again, thinking that I will probably never see Dima again.

Even if we both return alive. Even if we return in victory, I'll never see him again. Dima is not one of those whom you could casually meet in the metro or at an Odesa beach. You can't meet him in Munich airport running between gates or in a Nizhyn commuter train. Dima, and those like him, return to their villages in the Chernivtsi region, get into an old tractor, and work hard on the fields and gardens until retirement age. And those like me will never travel to that village to visit those like him. Such things happen in life.

So Haysyn It Is

Who'd have known that in three weeks I would manage to love them. To love them and to accept them. In the way in which people love and accept their own children, with all their shortcomings and transgressions. They are now almost family. Though this love must still be tested by time, but we don't have time. We are sitting in the tent, swooning from fatigue and sun, waiting for the "buyers," who would take us to their regiments, put us in Humvees and trucks and drive us to the unknown steppes and distant checkpoints. But Kostya, the assistant commander, rushes in with his characteristic industriousness, and suddenly utters my last name.

"You got ten minutes. Pack up. To the training ground. The ninth battalion."

This way of talking sounds like a sentence, as if I just received ten years of imprisonment without the right to appeal.

"And what about them?" I wave senselessly towards my fellow Kyivites. "They are with me!"

"They are not with you," chuckles Kostya, choking on cigarette smoke.

And so begins the spectacle of goodbyes. Nobody had ever hugged me in this way before, or shaken my hand, or wished me a safe return home as these people had... Andriy wishes that I will find my "soulmate" there. Yura, a construction worker from Vynohradiar, a neighborhood in Kyiv, tells me to never, under any circumstances, let myself be taken prisoner. Vasya prophesies that I will meet a "Gypsy," as we call her, who will change my life. "My God, what Gypsy, what prisoner," I think, running towards the training ground with the same Polish backpack and red Deuter backpack. I run and kick up sand with my boots, and for the last time I breathe in the sour smells that drift from the kitchen. Near the admin building, the newly drafted are hanging out. Heat lingers over the training field. My heart jumps because of the uncertainty and the absurd fear of being crucified here, on this training ground. "The chosen" are picked up by a young lieutenant whose face has not yet seen a razor, probably a recent college student. He takes us by train to Rivne station. Forty soldiers mixed with people who are going to their dachas fill up the commuter train. At one of the stations, most people exit. I sit down. Across from me sits an old man. He's dressed in a rugged uniform, has a military beret on, and he wears it like a criminal. His fingers are covered in tattoos. At the end of the car a soldier who looks like a street urchin from the 1920s, takes off his boots and puts his bare unwashed feet directly onto a bench across from him. He grimaces, but I take it, this is his way of smiling. Several soldiers stand near the window and look at the Volynia landscapes with sadness in their eyes, almost puppy-like. The dill and strawberries are fragrant in the baskets of the dacha folks.

At the train station in Rivne the soldiers all disperse among the local shops and bars. In the waiting area of the train station our voices sound loud and it's impossible to tell the words apart. Near the generator there's a line of those wishing to recharge their phones.

"Where're we headed, Sir?" I ask, at what seems a good moment.

"Haysyn," he says.

"And our battalion, where does it stand?"

"Haysyn and Partisans."

I look at Google Maps. I know where Haysyn is. I find out Partisans is in the south Kherson region. Oh well, so Haysyn it is. Not exactly the cradle of the Cossack army, but in its time the city had Magdeburg rights, the privileges of city autonomy in the Middle Ages. Whereas some of the Cossack army cities did not.

It is four hours until our train. I'm sitting in the waiting area drinking kefir. One bottle, two. What did I miss these past days? Kefir, of course. What I didn't miss were the shooting exercises, midnight revelry and forced marches, the same jokes told for the umpteenth time, drunken quarrels, radio that transmits Russian pop, and the heartburn that I experienced again after many years. But I did miss kefir. Just like a sailor in the Middle Ages must have missed veggies.

I go outside for a smoke. The sun is already hiding behind the train station. Across, near the blue phone booths, ordinary city pigeons take lazy strolls. Near the *marshrutkas*, the drivers dressed in similar-looking T-shirts hang out. A man approaches me; he looks like a young taxi driver.

He speaks softly, asks me about the service, and honestly admits that he himself is afraid to enlist. At least he offers to buy me cigarettes. I listen, diligently answer his questions, and refuse the cigarettes.

A few feet from me several of our soldiers are so drunk that they can barely stand on their feet. The lieutenant pleaded for us not to drink, he practically begged us. Well, so we put the drunk soldiers in line on the floor of the waiting area. I buy another liter of kefir. For later. The arrival of our train is announced.

They say Haysyn has its own dairy.

Thirty

After twenty-four hours in Haysyn I get a leave to go to home to Kyiv. However, in a day and a half sergeant Zeleny orders me to return: we are going to the mythical town called Partisans. Another unexpected twist is added on to the situation: I carelessly drank too much cold kvass and suddenly developed a very high fever. Our medics find out the specifics: 41 centigrade and they suspect acute strep throat.

"So what, you're staying behind? No way anyone will take you to Partisans with such a fever," says Sasha the doc, an overweight guy of about twenty-five. To be honest, I don't want to go to Partisans, but to stay behind with two sergeants and an officer on duty in Haysyn, and then to look for my base in Partisans and my regiment by myself is even less appealing. So I write a memo that in the case of my untimely death I'm the only one who should be blamed. I receive three pounds of pills and some shots of painkillers into my butt, I sign off, and in the morning with the same high fever I take off for Partisans in one of three old-style buses.

My path is my pain. My pain is my problem. Besides, I've already signed the memo. Every two hours I swallow some ibuprofen and spray my throat with something that smells weird, making my fellow passengers look at me funny. From time to time, my consciousness grows dim: I either fall asleep or faint. "God," I say, addressing not so much God but my own inner voice. In ten hours I will turn thirty, I am on my way to some place called Partisans, in the south of the country, and my base is most likely some cluttered and impoverished checkpoint with snakes and darting steppe lizards. But I am my own doc on top of everything – I just signed the memo.

From time to time we stop for repairs because the engines overheat. We sit for a long time in the shadows of the willows that grow along the roads. We throw cigarette butts and empty water bottles into the tall grass. We are given dry rations called "Visit," and I finally understand what it is and why nobody eats it. Escape, I start thinking about escaping. But with this kind of fever I will be lucky if I make it to the closest hospital. I dive into my dreams again. I dive into the sweltering air, grab it with my mouth, like a fish that was thrown onto the hot asphalt pier. I wake up because somebody is shaking me.

"Kherson!" I hear: "Kherson."

There is so much joy in this voice, as if we are passing the Grand Canyon and this is the only chance to see this natural wonder.

"I am from Kherson!" the voice adds.

"I'm so happy for you," I say to myself and again sink into something much like quicksand, falling through the clouds made of resin and the sandy fog to the very bottom of consciousness, from where there is no return and where there is no forgiveness.

"Home!" one of the officers exclaims. The gate opens, and we enter the territory of what used to be a giant grain elevator.

I come to in a quickly assembled tent. My stuff is lying near the entrance. A tall and proper sergeant from the locals tells us to line up. The watch shows 7 a.m.

We are distributed into five platoons. Along with five soldiers, I am taken by a dude called Seryoga with the nickname Katso. On the way to the barracks he informs us that hooch and theft are punished mercilessly. I almost faint from exhaustion. I choose a bed and quickly become acquainted with my new mates. In ten minutes we are taken out to listen to a concert brought over by the volunteers, who have driven so far to sing us some songs. I sit down on the grass, sparse from many footsteps, striving to find some shade, but this place has no such thing in principle. Three older guys in old uniforms are singing Afghan campaign songs, in Russian. I sway as if I am a little boat in the open sea. I hear in the distance the choir of cicadas singing in the background. I try to get up and to walk towards the barracks, but my legs give in. On the lyric "and he left, without having met the first spring, and he returned home in a soldier's zinc coffin" I fall, and hear above me the voice of Seryoga "Katso": *Medics!*

"Happy birthday, dude. Isn't this how you dreamed of celebrating your thirtieth birthday?"

Class Conflict

It takes me forever to become part of any new community. Not an easy process, I'd say. My usual place is over there, behind the curtains. This is me sitting there. And watching. Maybe, it seems to everybody that I am constantly on my phone, browsing Facebook or reading the news, but I'm not. I am watching, studying, and analyzing. I choose my service mates. I choose those who will be able to save my life.

I remember how difficult it was for me to approach the workers who were drilling a well in the yard of our dacha and to offer them coffee and sandwiches. What was I supposed to say to them? How will they perceive me, with my refined Ukrainian, wearing white and orange Adidas shoes and a blue sweater?

"Hi guys! How's it going? Maybe you want some coffee? Which cheese do you prefer on your sandwiches: Gouda or Emmental? I say the weather is great today!"

This sounds like a scene from the prose of the Russian émigré writer Sergei Dovlatov. "I remember I shouted out something terribly intelligent-sia-like: *Maestro, you are forgetting yourself!*" Normally, simple working-class men and boys treat me with opposition, class distrust and skeptical gaze.

In reality, I am rather uncomplicated myself, and I love simplicity. I can also use expletives. At times, I can only use expletives. I can drink a shot. I can eat simple potatoes with bacon. But I can also converse about Chaadayev and Hertzen, the nineteenth-century Russian writers.

A new community means attention and a scrutinizing look. This is not just distrust due to social class, this is distrust in general. All encompassing, on the level of such concepts as life and death. How can they be sure that you, who are so calm and quiet, will not unload your gun's magazine into them at night? Or maybe you are a separatist to begin with. Whom am I looking for? Whom am I fishing for, like a fisherman at a pond? A friend?

A "brother in spirit?" A human whose jokes I will be able to get? A person whose vocabulary will not expose him as an ex-criminal? In my search, I am pragmatic. I need protection.

I need trust. Maybe experience, too.

I don't know them. I don't know this dream team yet. I am only sitting here and watching them closely. To which one of them should I entrust my life, whose children will I baptize, whose retreat will I cover. They are also watching me. And I must irritate them to no end, by staring at my phone, by constantly drinking coffee and smoking, and by speaking refined Ukrainian. This is what is called distrust for one's social class. But it will all go away after the first shot and, of course, after potatoes with bacon. Bacon brings people closer together. Whether everybody believes it or not.

Somebody Else

I have been to such small towns only in passing. Somewhere in the Crimea, between Bakhchysarai and Simferopol, they fit into the landscape so well that they are perceived as part of it. It is at first hard to see the dry grass under the fence and the yellow houses made of limestone. Apricots, wild roses, automobile tires dug into the ground, dry soil, an outhouse with walls covered with black tarp, a broken Minsk fridge under the slate tent. Our battalion is located on the territory of an abandoned grain elevator. There are a lot of snakes and snails here. The snails are huge, the size of a walnut; the snakes are small and wavy. Across from the elevator are a church and a mosque. Sometimes children approach the gate and shout, "Glory to Ukraine," and ask for money.

If I am not on duty, I go to bed at 9:30 p.m. and wake up at 5:30. At 6 a.m. everybody wakes up, so this way I have half an hour to enjoy total silence. Thirty minutes of not hearing the shouts and loud conversations of other soldiers. Silence for me became a deficit and a delicacy of sorts. I only get it in homeopathic doses, and I relish it, sucking on it slowly as if it were chocolate or Parmesan.

To have personal space no matter what is an important habit. To learn not to hear the surroundings is a skill that takes weeks to develop. To sleep through loud platoon life is the highest level of mastery. Yet reading for me is something I can only do when it is quiet, therefore in five weeks I only read one and a half books.

Despite the fact there is more than enough spare time, reading becomes a luxury. Even writing comes easier, because it's a different way of concentrating. This is why I gladly agreed today to stand guard. Being alone there is an opportunity for solitude. It means some extra hours of silence and concentrating on myself, and thus, a chance to write longer stories and to think on a larger scale, and not in small increments of time. Edik is another guy on the same post. He is turning forty-five today. At night he complains about fate and tells me that life is generally shit. He goes on talking about his wife, his enemies, mutters something about the snipers. Overall, it seems that the cause of all his rambling is lack of sleep. Then Misha comes. For a few hours he tells me about the life of a loader for the Youth Market. According to him, it is impossible to find good work in Kyiv. For one spot as a security officer at the supermarket there are ten applications.

I am not interested in his problems, so I turn around and head off to walk around the territory and wander in the dark. At this time when everybody is still sleeping and you are walking around, stepping on mulberries and snails, and breathing freely. The thing is, you feel like an observer of your own life. Or, on the contrary, you view your life as somebody else's. There is something deviant about it, something sickly. You are embracing everything at a glance – your behavior, the motivation of your actions, old habits, which you are trying to adjust to your new role. But ultimately it is not you who is observing it but somebody else, somebody whose life you are living.

The other thing I think about is sleep. There is nothing sweeter than thinking about sleep: how your guard duty will be over, how you will take off your worker's jacket and boots, how you will jump up to your top bunk of the bunk bed and fall asleep.

And the air starts lightening up. There's no more than twenty minutes left of my guard time. The change of guard show up earlier and lets you go, tells you to go to bed. After all, you have been on duty all night long. And I do go, take off my uniform, take off my boots, lay down my weapon, jump on the bed, but I can't fall asleep. Today is Sunday, and the bell ringer starts the canonical ringing. Maybe he is congratulating Edik on his special day. Or me, on being the outsider here on this godforsaken territory in the glorious town of Partisans.

Camp

We arrive at the grounds of an abandoned children's summer camp. Along the overgrown alley there are emaciated cement skeletons of buildings without windows and doors like the post-apocalyptic houses of Prypyat, the town most affected by the Chernobyl disaster. Somewhere there, beyond the buildings and the planted trees, the Sea of Azov begins. From the shore you can see Arabat Spit and the little island of the Azov-Sivash nature preserve. About three miles north there is the town of Frunze, just as poor and touched by misery as most towns around here.

Camp. Our new shelter, a colorless fortress of the first assault brigade. We disperse around the buildings and settle in the rooms. On the pale pink walls we see the remnants of children's creativity: drawings, hearts and stars cut out of paper, sentences about eternal friendship and endless love. We bring in beds and other stuff, pick up broken tiles and cement, sweep away the trash, connect the generator with the wires to our field cable. Those punished for minor offenses are digging the outhouses and pits. The locals come on motorbikes, look at us, get acquainted, assure us that they are loyal to the "new Kyiv government," and offer to bring food and alcohol and, if we want, to bring us to meet girls.

They also advise us not to wear sandals because there are more snakes here than on Snake Island.

Immediately in front of the buildings, there is a huge freshwater lake. The guard allows us to fish. But only with fishing rods, not with explosives.

We have entered a new stage. It seems to us we belong only to ourselves, and commanders, who are higher in rank than our platoon leaders, have no idea where we are at the moment and what we are up to. In the first days of our stay one of the officers brings over his son, a boy of about ten. The platoon divides into groups according to interests. Some spend hours fishing, others in the town of Frunze. Some discover the healing properties of Azov mud; the mud moves because of all kinds of living organisms as soon as you scoop some up in your hand.

In the evenings, we organize a snake safari. There are hundreds of them. In the evenings, they crawl out to hunt, destroying spiders and snails, ruining bird nests, and coming over into our kitchen and munching on food scraps. You better be careful and not joke around with them. Every visit to the latrines can become your last. Their size amazes us: they could easily extend a few feet. Sometimes they crawl on to the walls of the buildings, to warm up their cold bodies, and hang down like tropical plants.

Forgetting the war and the service in general, I suddenly feel light and happy, as if this Azov heat, the sun, the mirror carps in the lake, action and sleepiness are but a continuation of our vacation to Crimea two years ago. Emptiness and emotional weightlessness rule here, and your thoughts are in a different plane of existence, ethereal and high above clouds, where the gods eat figs and grapes and wash them down with sweetened Massandra wine.

And the weapons, it seems, are but a decoration put on you, much like a sword displayed on special occasions. And the night shift duty is but a late dinner that slowly turns into a session of smoking hookah and long conversations until the sun rises over Donbas. After that Leonidovych, the commander of the fourth platoon, will call you for breakfast.

War Is Not Interesting

War is not interesting. Even when they tell us that in a week we will be going to the front, we are not particularly interested and don't discuss it much. As for practicing shooting, that we do like, to get our way around some tactical strategies or just to work out with weights. We are always pleased, but we have no desire at all to talk about war.

Undoubtedly, each of us has this or the other scenario running through his head. We collect our first aid kits, little by little, piece by piece. It very well may be that some are working on their will. Our battalion is so ill-equipped that we could pass for a guerilla unit. Not all soldiers have enough uniforms, most have not received their salary for at least a month and a half. It is three miles to the closest store, and cigarettes are already a universal currency. The families are left behind, but their problems travel along with the soldiers: money issues, illnesses, affairs. Some are even in the process of getting divorced long distance. So, as you can see, war is not interesting.

Yet we are ready to be at war. Even barefoot. Let them throw us to the front as soon as possible. Waiting is more unbearable and pressing. Everybody feels the danger that creeps after each of us like a loyal dog, but we take it lightly, jokingly. If we must be at war, then so be it. And if I kick the bucket, well, then, I do. It is most important to have enough cigarettes. And cheap noodles.

War is not interesting. The stories of those who have already looked it closely in the eye are just as casual as stories about exes.

Soldiers are much more interested in finances. Some start collecting scrap metal: old carcasses, metal sheets, rusty wires. They say that at the front the supplies are better: the reflector gunsight. And, while we still have a chance, one should go fishing, or finish that tattoo, or write that short story. While we still have a chance, time, and desire. Soldiers are not interested in the war, and their need for it is even less than their interest. The same is true about their families, or the inhabitants of Donbas, passers-by in big cities, farmers in the Kherson region, fishermen in Odesa, shepherds in the Carpathians, electricians in Rivne, teachers in Nizhyn, chemical plant workers in Cherkasy.... But surely there must be those who are interested in this war? And, most importantly, those who need it?

Imitation

Lazurne, a small town in the Kherson region.

We are given five cans of meat and two loaves of bread.

"You will be guarding the object, the platoon, and ammo," said the platoon leader.

"Understood."

Lieutenant Edem meets us in the yard.

"Is this your nickname?" we ask. "Edem" in Ukrainian means "Eden."

"No, it's my name."

Edem is a contractor with a child-like face without eyebrows. He has a balding spot in his reddish hair.

"So what should we do?" we ask him.

"Most importantly, do not get trashed," he pleads. "Well, and guard the place, too. These acres of land are yours."

The only thing the previous platoon that was stationed here was guarding was their alcohol. If they even had any, that is. If they ever considered storing it.

We approached the gig in a responsible and somewhat dramatic manner: guards, full equipment, all the ammo. In the case of intrusion we put them face down. Among us there are some who especially value this way of problem solving.

Though as far as I am concerned, this doesn't solve any problems. It's more like it creates some extra ones.

We are standing literally in shit, and this means near the sewage collector. The cistern comes by every half an hour or so. It raises dust, it makes us depressed and irritated. Why so much? In such a tiny town? Oh, that's right, tourist season at the seashore – melons, greasy meat pastries, new wine… At night we are surrounded by the sharp odor of excrement. The heat during the day melts our brain, the flies drive us nuts. The waves of hot air flow over the steppe, as if over a gas stove.

Nobody can shake off the sleepiness. Only cold soda saves us during the day, and cold beer in the evening.

"Special reserve" means that we are being used whenever they lack hands. Five, six, twenty people at a time. Guarding the buildings, holding the rear positions, imitation of military service. The men want to go east, to the front lines. To sit here in the reserve is shameful, and to squander time doing nothing is impractical. Some invent the front lines for themselves right here and now, guided by their inner pain, disregarding the locals and misunderstanding the civilians. Maybe they have a reason. Maybe this is fair. These couch strategists don't really know what war is like, they've never seen women's and children's corpses, or heard the hissing of the mines. Some of us have already felt what the war is, in full. They have it the worst. Less than a mile from us is the embankment. The vacationers stroll there, warmed by the sun. They wear patriotic T-shirts. They brought their wives and children with them. Or lovers.

They are tipsy from drinking cheap cocktails at the local bars. The marketplace smoothly transitions into the overcrowded and dirty beach. Shrimp tails, beer caps and greasy plastic stick out from the sand. From looking at large quantities of rather ugly naked bodies, the canned meat that we eat for breakfast causes nausea. Run, run away from this place...

We are standing on shit. We are surrounded by steppe and the skeletons of unfinished resort hotels. Dry grass prickles our feet through our Crocs. Boredom, heat, reserve. In a week we have not swam in the sea even once, but every night, during the night duty, we look at the starry night skies asking ourselves awkward questions: What are we here for? Were we all taken away from our families, mines, nightclubs, vegetable gardens, and factories just so that we could guard these acres of the steppe? Why do we have to be here together with the contractors, who are at least paid on a daily basis?

Of course, the commanders console us: you will be on the front lines soon. At the end of August. Or in September. And for now, you are here. Get stronger, you will need your strength. The days flow by slowly like waters of the lake. During the day we wear shorts and T-shirts, at night—a uniform and ammo. Finally they bring us our salary, part of it: now we can afford vegetables, leafy greens, eggs. Volunteers bring us a box of cookies, friends procure coffee and tea. Plums have ripened. The contractors bring fish: we can make fish soup. We find wood for the fire: chop down the buckthorn.

We listen to jazz, rap, the Russian bards Vysotski, Novikov. We are serving our country, or, more precisely, we are imitating service.

The sounds of dance parties come to us from the embankment. Our food is almost cooked over the fire, and the trailer is filled with hot draughts. The sun is slowly sinking behind the hill that stands between us and the sewage collector. The mosquitoes are buzzing, the flies are getting glued to us. We're lying in our beds and wishing that the summer would come to an end. Such a new summer for us all, a summer like a dream, a long winter dream.

A Green Chinese Tractor

For the third day in a row we are being relocated all over the steppe, from one place to another. No goal. No explanation provided. We came to one location, stayed there for a while, left for another. This has been going on for sixty-five hours on end. The bus, packed to the brim, is staggering at the curves of the road and stops from time to time to cool the engine down.

We exit from the salon to take a leak, to smoke or to stock up on energy drinks or light alcohol at the local stores. Today we have crossed the Askania-Nova nature preserve twice. We cut corners via the farmers' fields with melon and watermelon plantations. At one of them the engine stopped.

The radiator was emitting thick white smoke. In the transparent skies a lonely peregrine falcon was flying. The irrigation system was slowly moving over the field. The owner of the field, upon seeing us on his land, got interested. He drove up to us on a green Chinese tractor that moved with the speed of a quadricycle bike.

"Hey you, guys," he greeted us in Russian, "What are we fighting for?"

"For your dog's dick," one of the soldiers answered, shaking drops of water to the ground.

"My point exactly," said the driver, getting visibly nervous. "But in more concrete terms?"

"For you, you ram," said the other soldier.

"But we've got no war over here," the driver was unrelenting. He was bald and red-faced, like an Irish seaman.

"So you will," said the sergeant with menace in his voice. "You want war? I will give it to you, you son of a bitch. You will run doggy-style all the way back to Mykolaiv. Got it?"

The farmer was visibly sweating, and his eyes were twinkling with fear and hate.

He spat loudly under his feet, demonstrating his fearlessness, turned around, sat back into the soft orange seat of his tractor, drove a few meters off, stopped and now was watching us from a safe distance.

After a while, we fixed the bus problem and started to drive, but stopped again in a quarter of a mile or so. The watermelon farm began. Huge watermelons lay very close to the road, tempting us. A few soldiers jumped out of the bus, quickly picking them and loading them into the bus, throwing them onto the mattresses and backpacks.

The farmer watched us from afar. He stood in the middle of the road crossing his arms across his chest. He would not dare stop us. He was watching silently, nurturing hate for us and sympathy for himself. I felt bad for him. The man was flabbergasted and shocked. Watermelon juice was streaming in his arteries, and his bald head was being warmed by the white sun of Kherson. I felt bad that we did not manage to work things out. The soldiers, with their usual rudeness, and the farmer, who so carelessly asked what we are fighting for. The correct answer to his question wasn't, of course, his dog's dick. And not even he himself. And it goes without saying that there is no war in Kherson. Instead there are watermelons. And a cowardly farmer in his green Chinese tractor with the license plate that begins with AH.

Keep Writing, Chekh

"Chekh, why are you pacing?" Sanya, my friend and commander, asks.

"And what should I be doing?"

"Go to the tent and write your book. That is an order."

Suddenly I realize that a lot of people expect a book from me.

My army comrades, and some of my commanders, and those who are not in the army – they all expect something. It's their expectations versus my responsibility. I am afraid to disappoint them. Afraid not to live up to their expectations, to miss something, to fail to mention somebody, to overdo and or to leave something unfinished.

"Write about all this bullshit," Katso says. "And write now, because later you will forget, get nostalgic and recall only the positive."

Each time something absurd happens, or idiocy of the highest commanders rises to the level of a tsunami, I immediately hear:

"Have you written about this? At least on Facebook? "

"Will you write about me?"

I will. I have a good memory. There's more than enough material. The characters are colorful, there are a lot of them, so many that I lose count.

But I can already hear exclamations of discontent: Why did you write about me in this way? Or about the army? And vice-versa: Why not about me, and why didn't you mention this or that instance?

I write using my phone. It's full of sketches, quotes, and observations. But my almost total integration into the system does not let me evaluate the situation critically, or to see the absurd and disturbing for what they are. Whatever could send me into a stupor or shock in my civilian life, I now see as normal.

The limits of cruelty are inevitably becoming broader, just like watercolors on a canvas. One starts to feel less and less pity towards fellow humans, and display more and more callousness and rudeness. One soldier today accidentally stepped on a kitten, it did not die then but it was obvious that, if left to live, it would have a miserable life. I calmly picked up a spade and said, let's go, I'll bury it, ready to go to the field. Later I realized that I was ready to finish the poor animal off. I was appalled at myself. Instead, we took the kitten to the doctor. The doctor did what he could, manipulating the animal's spine. It seems like the kitten will live. This little episode suddenly showed me with astonishing clarity that with time I will probably not be able to write adequately about what I felt and saw. One cannot be a detached observer here: objectivity is latent, subjectivity distorted.

Of course, I'm still capable of feeling surprise or rage. I still can't accept some things. At times I feel like talking about these experiences, making them into a finite narrative, but I restrain myself just in time from writing the superfluous, from implicating my friends and comrades, from busting the system in which I've been living, and from exposing too much.

But maybe I'll still write about all this. Later: in a year or in ten. I don't know whether it will be for better or for worse. Maybe, it'll be an absurd army-style piece, appropriately crude. Am I in shock? Or in stupor? I don't know...

Betrayal / Victory

Our country is at war. And we must steer the information war, we can't just talk shit about our army on Instagram.

This is the duty of our deputy platoon leader – to lecture us on betrayal and our Instagram. This is what he is here for, and our obedience and dedication to pain, hunger and thirst are his daily bread.

"If something is amiss, you can write a report," our deputy platoon leader continues. Write a report and we'll look into the issue. But it's much easier to put the information straight on Instagram than write a report, and it's a much more fruitful approach anyway. Reports have the unfortunate propensity to fly among the tables of the administrators and to quietly disappear into the heights of the atmosphere.

There are thousands of aspects, angles, hues and nuances of betrayal and the pseudo betrayal. Some soldiers or officers send home the bags of the volunteer help brought for the army. In the meantime, they walk around in torn shorts. Others are happy to have received their new Canadian winter boots even in July. Some spend their own money buying the necessary things for their squad, while others drink away their salary in the first days of having received it.

Some have three types of uniforms, others were not given any. At times for a whole week we receive great food, not worse than homemade style restaurants in Kyiv, but then next week we only have kasha. Today our commander was in a great mood and joked during formation, gave out awards, and tomorrow he will tell everybody to go fuck themselves sideways.

And then the blogger woke up in a bad mood and wrote in his Instagram that the commander is an idiot and a thief. And the commander, maybe, decided to open up some stuff sent over by the volunteers and to give it to soldiers. But then he receives a phone call. They ask him, "What's going on?" He responds, "Not much, here I give the soldiers cigarettes, a uniform, and toilet paper." Or, perhaps, a platoon leader got into a drinking cycle. Or, on the contrary, the soldiers are the ones drinking, and the leader runs around from one soldier to another trying to nurse them to some more or less appropriate state.

And in the neighboring platoon the soldiers did not receive sleeping bags because the platoon leader forgot and didn't send the request in time. The next day, a soldier burned down a tent. The others were arrested for something. Tomorrow this soldier has to go to the front lines, and he cannot tell one weapon from the other, because his instructor was a month away from the end of his own service, and decided not to do his job.

And the commander sits and daydreams about the status of the participant of military actions while his soldier sits and daydreams about a woman and new tanks.

And the soldiers walk around and ask to be let go either to the village or to town. One needs to go to the drug store, the other to the strip club. And everybody around is a traitor. One likes canned meat, because at home the best he ate was bread with mayo, and the other has stomach cramps from it. One takes five rolls, the other none. To one it seems that he is doing a huge favor to the state by just lying around in the tent, the other silently works on an old truck, picking at it as if he were a dentist working on somebody's teeth, trying to make the broken machine work.

One platoon leader takes his men on a run every morning, the other lets them sleep until 8 a.m. In both platoons there are disgruntled soldiers unhappy with the arrangement. And of course there is a hidden blogger who randomly writes all of this down. Or a writer. Or a journalist. Or the brother of a deputy. Or the brother of a journalist. Or the brother of both the journalist and the deputy.

And some media will reprint this writing with the hashtags betrayal and victory. Some readers will see love in it, some will see hate in it. Depending on your sight, you will see one or the other.

Life and death. Prayers and curses. Eros and Thanatos. The collective and the private. Manipulations, distortion of the facts, devaluing the truth, instant translation via Google Translate and hundreds of comments from the same IP address. This is all the manifestations of them, the betrayal and the victory, they march step in step with the soldier who has an Instagram account.

And, by the way, we always get plenty of bread rolls, which I personally consider an unquestionable victory.

Camouflage Cockroaches

I've always loved Kyiv. At times more, at times less, but the feeling that it's my city never left me. Kyiv inspired me, irritated me, empowered and disempowered me. It was my Kyiv, my city, my capital. Ninety days of military service. I hadn't been home in a month. This is not too much and not too little, but enough to grow unaccustomed to the civilians and to forget a civilian version of the self: how you dressed in shorts and sneakers, how you ran around the city's streets and lived an uneventful life, taking to heart your everyday troubles and the angst of writing. And suddenly I receive several days of leave.

To see family, to catch up on sleep and to pick up stuff collected by the volunteers for our platoon. My first impression of Kyiv, when I returned from the training field, was very negative. I failed to perceive the most usual and logical things, as if I had a thick fog in front of my eyes. Why aren't all men wearing uniforms? Aren't we a country at war, aren't soldiers dying on the eastern front? Instead, all you see are billboards with the ads for a new hamburger place. "A wild night, open-air! Don't miss the hottest rhythms of this summer!" "Haven't you been at the seashore?"

I have. But I didn't like it. My friends would invite me to parties, but I'd just say, what party? Thank you, but another time. "O Kyiv, I understand you, but I do not accept you. For now... Perhaps, some time should pass for me to forget the barrack humor, the smells of the field kitchen, the dust, and the drunken shenanigans of my army buddies?"

A few days after my return I could not even muster the strength to leave the apartment. I could not look at the people in supermarkets and the metro. I had a problem with their carefree attitude. The bearded hipsters in lumberjack shirts irritated me. I thought of expensive cars only in terms of their potential use for my platoon.

We call such bugs "cockroaches in one's head." They've been drafted, just like I was. This is my experience, my perception of civilian life. And yes, it is distorted and subjective. All these people around me, they are really lovely, at least the majority. Some actively help the army. I'm sure that many of them have family members or close friends in the Ukrainian Military Forces. In the evenings they go to buy medicine in order to fill first-aid kits, or make masking nets for the soldiers. And if necessity arises, they will give their all.

Maybe they even pray for the guys who right now are sitting in the dugout somewhere near Krasnohorivka.

But my camouflaged cockroaches, who are dressed in the worn uniforms covered with holes, or with rubber shoes or old New Balance sneakers on their feet, are not pleased: "Everyone hide!" A day goes by, then three, then five. I get out of the house more often. I wear shorts and sneakers. My platoon is far away, six hundred kilometers from here. And I am here. And it is good to be here.

This is my Kyiv, my streets on which beautiful and kind people walk. And it seems that there is no war. I try not to think about the fact that in two weeks I will have to return to my platoon, and in another week or so, to set out to the east. I finally get into everyday problems. I finally start to take interest in what needs to be fixed in the house. The angst of writing returns too. A few meters from me, my son is watching a cartoon about Peppa Pig. I opened the Word file with my unfinished book, watched soccer, met with extended family…

Passing by the Vokzal'na metro station, I catch upon myself the looks of the soldiers, exhausted and burnt with the sun and gunpowder as they enter the metro. Of course: I am wearing sneakers, shorts, and a happy-go-lucky look. How can they know that in a few days I will return to them, and I'm one of them?

That we are together. It's not that I can nag them and explain that we are bound by the same thread and that in our heads the same music is playing and that my sneakers are but an artifact from my previous life, to which I will certainly return. But in the future. This is my Kyiv. Here one has a good life, here my family lives. Light August wind, pleasant music and tasty cheese from the supermarket – all of this is also here. Everything is as it always was. Just as it was when these soldiers had already been drafted, when they sat in dugouts and died, and I was still interested in new burger places and the hottest rhythms of the summer. Everything is as it has always been. But every night now I dream about the army.

Long T-shirts

Toilet paper. It sounds very prosaic. The army jokes about long T-shirts are already yesterday's news, but they are still around whenever the issue of the toilets is brought up. Especially if these bathrooms really do lack toilet paper.

We found out later who the culprit was. Our rations manager decided to add to the food three times the norm of fats, so we receive enough calories and were not hungry after field training. We received enough calories but immediately ran to the bathrooms. The whole company for two weeks straight was filling up the pits with badly digested kasha. For some reason, we were sure that this was because of the steppe dust, which mixed with our food.

I even came up with a joke: our task was to fill up all pits with shit, and only then would we be deployed east. I will add that the joke became popular among the soldiers. In the meantime, along with the catastrophic situation with defecation, the strategic stock of toilet paper was disappearing at an alarming rate.

And finally shit hit the fan. Here I have to mention that due to joint training with American and Moldovan troops our training field was surrounded by the National Guard, so we could not really get out of the tent in time.

An American soldier shouldn't see a drunken and badly clad Ukrainian army soldier. This is our private matter, hashed out in the kitchen.

The Ukrainian infantry resembles the homeless kids of the 1920s, and their nomadic dwellings are cluttered and poor. God forbid some of our Western allies will see a slob wearing a faded uniform and rubber slippers, and carrying a plastic bag that sports a tea ad but contains bottles with something much more intoxicating. It was therefore decided not to let us out. Not even to buy cigarettes or toilet paper. Only officers were allowed to go, and only beyond a certain rank.

So at first we used the patriotic newspapers sent to us by volunteers. That was the army press that wrote with strained pathos about the heroism of our troops. Paperback mystery novels also went well. Some people really took to cutting T-shirts into small pieces.

A little later when such a prosaic issue as toilet paper became a matter of overwhelming importance, we (me and my two buddies) decided to go and look for the headquarters officers so that we could all find a solution.

The first person we met was the chief of headquarters. Captain (who had only been the chief officer for a week) looked at us in consternation and didn't know what to do: to get mad that the common soldiers dared to come to him with such a question, or to really provide help, and thus to establish his reputation as a benevolent authority who is also a soldier's best friend.

Finally, it was decided that he will go and look for the deputy commander responsible for supply delivery. The captain ran between tents, stumbling over sacks with stuff, stopped officers and asked them if they saw the deputy commander.

Then the object of the search turned up; he happened to be just passing us by. When asked if he could spare several rolls of toilet paper he rolled his eyes, said they had no paper, and that the soldiers should suck it up. He also repeated the joke about long T-shirts. Aren't we mobilized? We tell him that the next T-shirts that we would use would be the ones he gave us. He was offended and left. This was the end of the first act.

At the same time, the deputy commander for technology was leaving the headquarters tent. He was a tall, gray-haired major with a dignified appearance. After he heard our explanation, he said to us, with reproach, that to make deputy commanders look for toilet paper was basically a damn indiscretion.

But he did give us two rolls from his personal stock. We could not help but note that this would not solve the problem in the global sense. He took me aside and told me discreetly:

"Guys, you are pigs, you know that, right?"

"Not quite, Valentynovych…"

"OK, I get it," he interrupted me, "That's enough. The only thing I want to ask for: don't write about it in that book of yours how you guys were making the deputy commander run around the training field looking for toilet paper. People don't need to know this."

"What, like, at all?" I got upset.

"Not while you are on active duty, no."

I agreed. I promised I wouldn't. But in a year, I said, I would recall this episode in my writing.

The next day Valentynovych personally brought over several packs of real toilet paper.

And the poor deputy commander, the captain, would turn away every time he saw us. It didn't work out for him to establish himself as authority after all.

It's All Good

I wish I had as much inner peace as Sanya B. He speaks quietly, his Ukrainian is pure, with a soft melody.

"It's all good, it could've been worse."

I'd get all worked up and point to our obsolete technology. I would almost shout. Such dinosaurs would do for the WWII era, but not for today.

But he says:

"If these trucks are here, somebody must drive them. Why not us?"

I would gesture actively and speak about our supplies, about the cheese that is brought not for us, but just for the commanders, about our synthetic uniforms that we must wear even in the 100°F heat, about the low quality boots. I looked at his feet. He was wearing black polished shoes without socks. Instead of shoelaces, he had aluminum wire. His pants were too long for him, so he cuffed the legs. Sanya had a beard. If you saw him from a distance, he looked like a hipster.

"You don't even have boots!"

"I do," he answered, laughing, "I wish I also had brains!"

We passed an American convoy. They had come here to the training field, for a planned training session. They were a graphic example of what an army should be and how it should be equipped.

"Look at their Hummers, look at their ammo, look into the eyes of this African American soldier with high tech gear." But Sanya calmed me down, saying that soon things will improve, that our supplies and gear would also be of the same kind. He said that once upon a time this soldier's grandfathers were discriminated against because of racism, but now everything changed, and the soldier had a personal porta-potty, and he was most likely reimbursed for any repairs or spare parts for his vehicle.

"We will have gear of the same quality," he said quietly.

"Our supply managers will never stop stealing cheese and canned meat. No matter how many volunteers would come and inspect our squads, the human factor will always prevail, that one that is a destructive force, a regressive drive, a lever of betrayal, an avant-garde of sabotage."

Sanya B. advised me to be more positive and to see only the pluses, otherwise I would worry myself to death.

"And after demobilization," he said, "start an investigation, but don't just do it halfway, really finish. The guys will support you."

I didn't answer. To start a direct confrontation with the commanders is not the easiest thing. Besides, we have no facts and no evidence, only interpretations and rumors.

We got out of the car, sat down on the grass, looking for shade, like puppies. We waited for a command. I crossed my legs and looked at the training field landscapes. It was yellow steppe, partially scorched by tanks. The tanks burned acres of land. There was not a cloud in the sky. Sweat was streaming down from under our metal helmets.

"You have it good," Sanya B. said. "You write something and then you feel better. And, at the worst case scenario, you've got friends, journalists, and they'll catch you if you fall. And I can't write, so I gotta look for positive things."

I got headphones from my pockets, turned on the first album of the band called Boombox. I was thinking about the positive. Dima got some cake and pastries from home. "Schulz" brought real Italian coffee. My uniform is made of 100 percent cotton, so it was easier for me to deal with the heat than for the others. Finally, they gave us sleeping bags.

Maybe that day I could do my laundry; we had a watermelon for dinner. I was in the army, a "priceless experience," I was in the army, and despite everything I served the Ukrainian people, fulfilling my duty towards the motherland. I got enough money, and I did not squander it on booze. I was being fed, my army buddies and the officers respected me, I had real army friends who would stand up for me to the end, I had a family and lots of wonderful people outside of the war zone, who were always ready to help.

And also the weather channel promises 28° Centigrade and occasional rain. And I could afford a new uniform or boots myself. Not to mention cheese. It was all good, it could've been worse.

PART II
Fall, Winter, and Spring Again

That Same Gas Station

We move slowly, repairing one or another APC, armored personnel carrier, every hour. We cover the fifty kilometers from Izyum to Slovyanska in six hours. Finally, close to midnight, we stop outside the city to spend the night at that very same gas station. It is legendary because hundreds of troops with technology and manpower have passed through it and continue to pass through it. That's where the first active checkpoint, is held by the National Guard. And of course, I see the bullet holes and shrapnel in the corrugated metal fences. We jump from our APC and run to the convenience store at the gas station. There's the indifferent sales girl, Oksana, and the clean gleaming toilets. Outside, by the gas pumps, I see a bunch of sleepy dogs. We buy some sausages. Afterwards, we talk to the National Guard soldiers who cajole a couple packs of ammunition from us, telling us stories of how unfortunate they are to be on duty at this dump.

"So, you are here, on the very outskirts of Slovyansk," we say, amazed. In response we hear a bunch of crazy stories, hard to believe, and for that exact reason, not at all disturbing. For example, how separatists throw grenades out the windows of moving cars. Right at peoples' feet.

We stand, smoke, and empty gas from the tanks of the two APCs, so that we can fill up others. These two are to remain here at the entrance to the gas station, the other four will drive off further. Where to exactly? The Captain doesn't even know. We weren't informed. They didn't tell us, they just threw us into the situation: to go to a populated spot in Volodymyrivka. And then? Who are we relieving? Where is it we are supposed to go? What is waiting for us? Who will die first?

Finally, close to two in the morning, at the conclusion of an electrifying caffeine high that is losing its effect, I crawl into the APC and shortly after I fall asleep. I would have slept like that at the edge of this very zone at this very gas station, until the war had ended and there wouldn't have been a surrender treaty signed by the enemy... But Sanya and Vlad wake me up, call me to breakfast. Sausages again. And we are all together, and the sun is so blinding, and the coffee so strong and with milk, it's as if we're at home, and our Coke is sweet and fizzy, and the tired National Guard soldiers are relieved of their posts and go to sleep – their trailers are there behind the gas station. They are heated with stoves and even have showers. We go further. South, toward Artemivsk, to the unknown defense posts, to the supporting positions, to new places that will reward us with new impressions like an amusement park would. The most important thing is to keep loving life, and have a sense of humor and the ability to delight in small pleasures.

We Are Here

This is the way that I imagined it up ahead, based on reading Vasil Bykaŭ or Konstantin Simonov, who wrote about World War II: bunkers as described there, trenches, a field kitchen. And somewhere, located up high – the enemy. He is definitely planning something. Of course, he is sending saboteurs. In principle, he is devious, brutal, cunning. Not like our simple boys with sincere faces and an unwavering sense of humor. It's true that the humor is usually dark and their faces sincerely reflect their despair. Here we are in our dugouts and positions, and there is the enemy. "The scout squads" sneak around the bush. They wipe away our inroads and replace them; at their high position they are responsible for calculating aim, storing mortars, and keeping track of the newly drafted, untrained soldiers, some of them separatist sympathizers.

This present situation – it is like that from those "inspiring" books about the greatness of bygone ancestral feats. Only none of this is very romantic. And it's hardly beautiful. And totally uninteresting. I don't know what justifies the poor quality of the army, the lack of essential tools, the commanders' indifference, but until the soldiers themselves start to care about what is most important, their actions will continue to be an illustration of "total betrayal" (at least in our case). For the older officers, the most important thing is to put a checkmark next to "helmet," "bulletproof vest," "backpack."

They only care for the equipment to have been "DISTRIBUTED." Their conscience is clear, and they can go back to earning money: officially and off the books. They have ways.

By the second day at absolute zero we aren't bothered by crossfire from adjacent positions, and even the realization that you can die at any moment becomes ordinary. Everyone around you talks only about the war. Weapons, tactics, the possible outcomes for both sides. By the way, about the weapons. There are enough. Enough to do battle. Without a doubt, everyone is tired of the war. Especially those who have spent eight or nine months under fire.

And those just taking their turns on the battlefield.

But everyone is ready to hold the position, however long it takes. So we stand our ground. Among the mice and fleas, in dirt and mud, without water or electricity, without good alcohol or sex, with cheap cigarettes, greasy food and carbohydrates. Without being able to wash more often than once in two, three weeks. We stand, trashing the news that comes to us from TV, and expressing disgust with everything: from the battalion commander to the president. But it's not for the commanders that we stand. We stand because retreat is not an option.

How could it be otherwise? It's true that some of the soldiers don't even leave their bunkers the first hours after taking up their position, finishing up the alcohol that was acquired on the third line of defense. Others, arm themselves with grenades and ammunition, becoming a walking human explosive. And some don't make it to the zone at all, check in to hospitals, go AWOL, or just refuse to serve in the ATO, or the Anti-Terrorist Operation, a euphemism for war.

And all the better for us. This means we will experience more of these dry hills of Donbas, colorful sunsets, bitter autumn winds, ammo, cramped yet reliable bunkers, hours on night patrols, twilight ghosts who prowl "the bush," nerve-wracking kilometers of bombed fields at the final line of defense, dried rations obtained in battle from our chief cook, packets of instant coffee, outlets for charging cell phones around a generator, drinking water while there is a serious shortage of water, sticky spider webs and mice droppings, and finally, vivid and frightful memories. But this will be sometime, somewhere, during a long and happy life after the war.

Guiding Principles

God and politics. These, from what I have observed, have the least influence in the army. Especially during war. In regard to God, all is clear (our society isn't sold on religious superstitions), but politics tends to be more of an individual thing. It is not surprising. Well, it's like sexuality or its absence. Of course soldiers talk about politics (as they do about God as well) but they don't argue over it. They can endlessly talk about this or that politician, popular only for a moment, or voice their opinions about some global geopolitical movement, but everything ends in empty rhetoric. No one wants to argue. When it comes to religion, it's pretty much the same.

My closest associates, and by that I mean my friends, have such opposing political beliefs that it would take an army to bring us together. So the army brought us together. It's easy to turn the talk about politics into something else. For example, to talk about sex. Opinions on this topic are also very individual, and no one will cross your boundaries, imposing their views. But this topic has one uniting factor – sex interests everyone. God, politics, and sex. In general, you can fight over other things. Preferences in food, various views of mortality, life choices. In the army they say: nothing here is yours except for the dirt beneath your nails. Leave all your religious and political convictions in civilian life. If you want, let's talk about weapons. Or tell me how much you miss your wife. But don't talk to me about God or politics. As a last resort, we can talk about sex.

Volunteers arrived to our positions from a political party that wants to be publicly known as "engaged" in the matters of helping the soldiers. They gave out political newspapers and propaganda. Soldiers voiced no opinions about the party or its leader. But everyone asked for newspapers to use to start fires in the stoves. A chaplain came to visit us. He arrived and quietly spoke: "If you want, we'll talk, if not – don't pay attention to me and may God keep you. I'm not here to thrust upon you what you don't want. And don't worry about the cigarette. I don't care." Prostitutes didn't come to visit us, but if there was the desire there were plenty in the city, weren't there? Well, you know, the ones that still have something to offer. The most important guiding principles concern everyday life and safety. A predictable routine is most important. It's that way in any closed society. You moved an object and didn't put it back in place. Everyone's working, you're resting. You ate and didn't clean up. You didn't wash up. Safety – is by far a more important issue. You fell asleep at your post. You got drunk there. You went to clean your weapon and didn't unload it or you unloaded it, but forgot to remove the magazine. You dropped a grenade launcher on your friend's head. This is forgiven but you can get an earful of much new stuff about yourself. You can get your teeth knocked out. You may be prohibited from using your weapons for a while.

But there is one principle that a fellow fighter will hardly ever forgive a friend for – theft. In all five months of serving no one ever stole anything from me. Nothing at all. Even though I always left everything out in the open and easy to take. It's better to offend someone's feelings about God, politics, or sex, than to steal something from a fellow soldier. It is moral death and the end for any regard for you as a person. It is a line you cannot cross. And everything becomes worse at the point of absolute zero. Conflicts too. People ignite like dried ambrosia. Everything hidden comes to the surface, like the stuffing in an army jacket. Then more everyday puzzles. The understanding of sex becomes very individualized, like a toothbrush or deodorant. Only five months have passed. For four of them – we're together. Some people joined us later. But it seems that this division, or even more this platoon, turned into an old group of friends, whose lives are consumed by alcoholism, chronic sickness, and chores. There isn't anyone to talk to about politics or about God. Sex? We can talk about sex.

Norms

There is that uncomfortable moment when some staffers arrive at our outpost wearing new shoes made by a local manufacturer and bringing the soldiers felt boots.

"Norms, norms, norms," the ministry for procurement of equipment defensively explains on the telephone. Usually your norms mean that you will freeze in your regular winter clothes in minus one weather. A typical soldier isn't interested in reading Facebook about the president's advisor or aide to the defense minister; he doesn't care about what is in the warehouses and what these new people in the cabinet are doing so that they can change the norms. An ordinary soldier has felt boots, a synthetic jacket with a lining, from which the filling is coming out, and with seams that almost immediately start coming apart. And the soldier has a couple pairs of socks and galoshes. Well, and thermal underwear, which on a whole isn't that bad, even though it doesn't keep out the cold. "And so, you're cold? That can't be! Everything is within the norms. Something isn't right with your sense of temperature, soldiers." So, if it's not right, it's not right. We'll try to change our sense of temperature. We really have a problem with that. And our stomachs are also not standard.

The commissioner from regional headquarters arrived. The verdict: the men are living like cattle. They said this exactly. But the commander contradicts it: a generator, a chainsaw, a rainproof cover for our bunkers, tools – we have everything. Aha, only this is all ours. The guys got together and bought a chainsaw with their salaries. And the other one – comes from the volunteers. Just like the generator, the tools, and the warm clothing. Just like the "night vision equipment," just like the binoculars, just like half the food, just like the electrical sockets, extension cords, and dishes. The battalion has a balance of rust and soot. The commissioner poked around, commented, ooed and ahed, and left.

And we? We carry on, as always. What do we want? What do we really want? They can't send us any further east. There isn't anywhere further to go. More to the south, there is only clay and greasy Donbas coal. The commanders can reduce the norms. For example, give out only one pair of socks for every two soldiers. Or, let's say, instead of a liter and a half of water a day they give us a quarter. And one hundred fifty grams of bread with sawdust. It's so that we don't get too much. Clearly, too much of the good stuff leads to sickness.

This is all so funny and so sad at the same time…I wonder, what will be next?

Absolute Zero

Today the chaplain blessed me. One hundred and forty days ago I would have replied: "I won't take part in your masquerade." And now I stood in one line with my friends and even crossed myself. Maybe because I was supposed to. Holy water dripped from my mustache and beard. I stood and thought, "Where am I and where is the military chaplain?" But everyone's here, in line next to the dugout. And somehow suddenly I felt so grateful that I had the chance to experience this. Precisely this. Together with my friends who are delusional religious believers. With this young chaplain to whom, I am sure, this seems like a military dystopia where he blesses weapons and killing. A blessing – is a placebo, the deep inner belief that the enemy's bullet will not find you and your weapon won't let you down. The world around narrows into a single place: the road, the dugout, the deployment, the field. Everything else is inconsequential. Overthinking, avoidance.

Probably it's the best time to evaluate how you've lived your life so far. It's also the possibility that death, *your* death, will occur in order for you to rid yourself of all the baggage of the accepted norms that you've so far stupidly ignored. I, myself, created this comfortable ignorance, everything in what I believe. *This* is what absolute zero really is. The boundary across from which lies madness and delusion. Beyond it there's only the end of thoughts, feelings, wishes. It's full immersion in yourself, freedom from wants and worldly needs. This is a total transformation into a different person, the one which I would've never been capable of becoming under any other circumstances.

From now on, I'm a forest creature, ha, a gypsy bum…

In the evening we sit around the fire, eating mashed potatoes, as always talking a lot, and laughing. And ten feet from us the chaplain is reading prayers by flashlight. Above us is a sky full of stars. Around us a quiet field and cold still air, and I think only about the fact that now I'm someone else.

Purified. Maybe it only seems that way, and maybe I want to believe I am. Faith isn't the worst thing to have, so as not to go crazy and not to keep questioning. It is also comforting, like the darkness, also unreal. Like the imaginary friend from childhood, who you tell your fears to, who you share space with in your childhood room, and who disappears as soon as you are grown enough to experiment with your body in the bathroom.

I get up and go to bed earlier than everyone else. Sleep is also a good thing. It also purifies and renews you so that you can perform like a machine. You lie alone in the half-darkness of the bunker and crawl half-asleep, looking at the pattern on the clay walls created by the sudden changes in temperature and humidity, looking at children's drawings brought over by the volunteers and at some huge piece of embroidery, with the image of large-chested woman that the guys hung up over the metal stove. There is something Roma-like about her features. Of course this wasn't intentional, it just happened: her long thin nose, dark eyes, full alluring lips. This is a woman that inappropriately came to live with us. She is also mobilized and traumatized by this war. Who is she? Someone's daughter? A random selection from among the sets of numbered embroidery. The mythical Roma Sara Kali, who wanders with chaplains on the front lines of Eastern Europe? That same Roma woman who was supposed to change my life? About her probable death and about her probable life. I think about my probable life and about my probable death. Will it be sudden, will it be here, in his damp bunker? But maybe I'll live for many more years and die somewhere in a pastoral landscape raising sheep and cattle? And the whole village will come to the funeral of the old man who rejected city life and moved close to knotweed and duckweed.

And how will they dress my body, to which patriarchal jurisdiction do the deacons who will sing beneath the willow at noon belong? And, most importantly, why are there boxes filled with junk that the former inhabitants left still on the shelves of this bunker?

I'm sleeping? But maybe, I'm just in a stupor. Absence and weightlessness. The night is dark and distant, and gunshots are felt rather than heard. In a few hours the guys will crawl back in, wake me with their usual question, "Chekh, are you sleeping?"

No, I'm not sleeping anymore. Of course I'm not asleep. How can I sleep when you, my dears, are so close? Again adjusting to reality, I finally wake up, sit up, wrapped in a blue synthetic sleeping bag. And new conversations begin, anecdotes from life, a lot of laughter. The kind that makes your stomach hurt. Four guys in two square meters, in a limited space and with a limited social circle – here only laughter brings about peace. That peace that we have so much of and so little.

Our Friends

Volunteers are our friends. Volunteers are the ones you wait for with earnest excitement. They arrive, like missionaries, bringing clothes, food, supplies that we really need, tools, and of course, tobacco products. Volunteers are cynical and determined. Sometimes – embarrassed. Some of them are uncomfortable that they are only bringing aid to the front, even though they don't live here and are not fighting. Others, on the other hand, look at you intensely, suspecting you of all army sins.

"Do you get drunk? Are you sure you don't get drunk? Maybe your friends get drunk? No? Well, what do you know?"

The volunteers are fearless. They come out to the very limits of the conflict zone. To where the enemy sniper's bullets reach. Shyly they ask for bullets as souvenirs or empty shells from grenade launchers for school museums. Volunteers are sensitive and vulnerable. They easily offend others and are easily offended themselves. They are offended when you ask them not to come because you have enough of everything. They are offended when you don't meet them at Outpost 20 but ask them to come to the headquarters. They are offended when you don't have the means to bring them to the defense position. They are offended when you don't give them enough attention and don't post a photo of a box of baked goods on Facebook. He carried this box from the Khmelnytskyi (Ternopil, Kirovorhrad) province. He promised his damn community that he wouldn't eat one pastry from this box, that it would reach there in good condition, together with their best wishes to the glorious soldiers and beloved defenders, and he took no less than ten photographs of the boxes with the soldiers. He kept his word. He brought the box. Gave it to them. Photographed it. And you don't want to put that photo on Facebook? Shouldn't people know about their heroes?

Volunteers are deliberate and meticulous concerning strategy, the algorithm of actions, classification, logistics, methodology, technology, and priority.

It means, yes, you have two defense positions. Six outposts. One hidden from view. Two of them are in sight of the other three. And the three shoot in all directions. You don't need four, but three binoculars and one television. Furthermore. Six tanks. Three getting repaired. One dug in. Two on patrol.

One toolbox is enough for you. But sometimes the volunteers are incompetent. Their souls are as clear as a Christmas morning. Their thoughts are pure, but negligence ruins all that sacred effort, all those blessed positives of volunteering, that have served as a healing communion for the nation for many a year. For example, among expired candies and cans filled with moldy raspberry jam, somehow they gave us three bags of women's clothes: synthetic blouses, belts, skirts, underwear, hoods from jackets. We unloaded all this stuff near the bunkers, thanked the volunteers and dispersed into our dugouts, bent over with shame and sadness. Together with these useless gifts the volunteers left a stash of newspapers promoting the election of one party. The papers together with the rags went to feed the fires in the metal stoves. The jam we used as a fermenting agent when making hooch in a plastic barrel.

The only thing we kept was a small red dress. We hung it on a hanger in the bathroom. What a reminder. What a testament to a miscommunication. What an army banner. Volunteers are our friends. Coal for the oven, rubbing alcohol, medicine, tools, glasses, clothes, shoes, cigarettes, home baking and canned goods, stands for high-caliber machine guns, camouflage nets. Hello from the Great Land. The stories about other divisions. Common acquaintances. A heroic photo. "No one is forgotten, nothing is forgotten!"

They transport in their pockets the wind of peace, on the tops of their automobiles is the earth that hasn't seen war for the last seventy years. They arrive tired and devastated. Maybe more so than we are. They saw more than we did. They bring us the love of families we don't know. The drawings of children that we will never see. The letters from women who had already cried their eyes out in the winter of 2014 when the government shot at the Maidan protesters. They are our friends. Thank you. Sincerely.

Light Gray Zone

The city. More precisely, part of the city. Dead, black, like a trooper's charred body. In the city about a hundred miners and just as many retirees live. The buildings are destroyed by artillery, the roads are mutilated by tank treads, all the windows are boarded up. The other part of the city is occupied. There, they say, there are epidemics of plague, typhus, and cholera. In the store they sell army rations, cheap cigarettes, chocolate, "Sasha" and "Diplomat" colognes, packaged fast food, and expired kefir. The sales woman says that today at the checkpoints they aren't letting the trucks with the groceries through. Maybe it will happen towards the end of the week. Maybe in the beginning of the month, if they come to some kind of agreement.

"An agreement about what?" I ask. "What can you come to an agreement about? This isn't occupied territory after all."

They have their reasons. Money decides everything. So it's understood. Money has always decided everything.

"And what if they don't come to an agreement?" I wonder.

"Then we'll come to an agreement," the sales lady says in a business-like tone.

She has a peaceful, gray face. Her husband was shot, not clear by whom, as a terrorist minion in the summer of 2014. Father and son work at the state mine. The coal contains a high percentage of ash and grease, and is of poor quality. The salary is two or three times lower than at Ukrainian Energy, Inc. but for a gray (someone calls it light-gray) zone, it is not bad.

In these light-gray zones, the roads are very particular. They are empty and cratered like the surface of the moon. You have to move quickly – you speed through shot-up sites. In general, quick drives through the destruction in Gazelles and "ambulances" became habit. And if our stay at this place becomes the norm, then these inhabited places seem absurd and unreal. I can't even believe that people live in these buildings. Their presence is revealed by the Sputnik antennas and the stove pipes that peek out from the wooden window frames. And you carry guns. You fly across the rough asphalt, you try to remember the surroundings, to carve these moments deep into your memory, you stop yourself because this is a terrible tragedy for other people who you have learned about. And then you go back to your station and rejoice in your bunker that over a month has become more dear to you than the tents at Rivne, the barracks at Haysyn and Partisans, a summer camp for kids abandoned outside Henichesk, the train at Lazurne, more tents at the Shyrokyi Lan training field.

And all these felt boots, solarium, generators, canned meat – all of this is petty. In front of me – the mine, a conveyor loaded with heaps of excavated coal, a local boy in military boots and sports pants, two old women are watching our Gazelle depart, the road dusty with a blown up military truck on the side of the road. Remnants of dried flesh in a burned-out cabin.

The Sound of the Train Station

Night falls unexpectedly. Twilight is almost imperceptible. An hour ago we were circling around the bonfire, drinking the leftover coffee from lunch, and now we're sitting at our outposts waiting for greetings from our enemy. Usually the night passes peacefully. The fall truce has all the signs of a truce. Metal isn't falling on our heads, and accidental gunshots from both sides are good for keeping up your skills. But the enemy comes closer, and whatever anyone says, we sense this. Even when the scouts go through the bush and then inform us that there aren't any traces, we know – the enemy is close.

The night is silent and scary. There are two of us at the post, and so, it's hard to come to a decision of what to do in case something happens. And all these horrific metal sounds that echo through the Popasna train station. *Uzht-uzht-uzht,* as if some gigantic machine is processing human souls. *Uzht,* and of course a voice. The voice of the dispatcher, that with the echoing spreads through the surrounding fields. The scary sound of the train station informs us that the enemy is close, that he is behind the bushes, there he has his sniper's lair, hiding, waiting until one of us comes out to a convenient spot for him. Boom! Silence again. Maybe a voice – female, strained – *Wow, wo – whoa!* Nothing to understand, except the fact that the dispatcher is earning her one and a half thousand hryvnias per month of a minimum wage. And then – silence. Sometimes a train with contraband can be heard passing in the distance. And then nearby – the sound of a fox. We are quiet. We get our weapons ready in the night, and the rustling and the crackling of dry branches. We fire from all barrels at the enemy! The residue of the gunpowder blinds our eyes, fills our ears, and we keep shooting, keep shooting. And over the top we throw grenades. Boom! We only see the shrapnel fly up in the sky. And the enemy is there, he didn't go anywhere. He is here now, encouraged by our fire and heavy hitting of the metal. After a moment, we hear over the radio:

"Who is that motherfucker shooting?"

"It's from the Taiha double-barreled shotgun," we answer, "putting the blame on another unit."

"Agreed."

Shultz jumps out from the dugout close to us. Comes over to us. He rubs sleep out of his eyes, grips the automatic weapon in his hands.

"Hey you, German, why did you come out?" we ask.

"It's a war, so I came to look."

"Don't just sit there, look around," we agree.

Shultz brings some coffee and some Italian pastries. We sit, chew, listen to the sound of the train station and sense the enemy; it seems he has almost crossed the line into our base. "Now the bitch will throw a grenade at us." But no, he doesn't throw it, only grumbles. "That's you, Markiz. You scared us." The cat came and is warming himself near the stove. And we warm ourselves, and of course, dream. Everyone has their own dreams.

Night Watch

War is a Lernaean Hydra with many faces. It gives someone the opportunity to get rich, to claim all of kinds of junk brought over by the volunteers, obtain the status of participation in military actions, or get a promotion to a higher rank. Someone unflaggingly directs the mobilization, following orders and of course not thinking anything through. Some become very anxious, curse the truce, and some wait for orders to attack. They don't need anything except mortars and grenades. And there are those who totally doubt whether their stay here is worthwhile. They are usually silent, but, when they began to speak, they open their souls and confess that they just don't understand why there is a war and who is fighting whom.

Over five months of serving, I've met more people than I have in the past five years. From these constant introductions, different personalities and fates, the faces and handshakes, everything gets mixed up in my head; people become like the figures of apostles in Prague's astronomical clock, passing by in black windows, replacing one another and leaving traces in my memory. Troops, doctors, volunteers. Either old men or totally young boys. Former criminals, miners, teachers, Maidan protesters and the latent revanchists. And among all these people only a select few have a definite opinion about the war. And even fewer know why they are here.

I didn't spend a lot of time thinking about this question and came up with a quick and totally banal answer. It turns out this wasn't painful at all. Why are we here? Because someone must be here. Whether there is a truce or not – it's not about that. We are here so that it doesn't go any further. It's not very important who: the locals or professional soldiers from the Russian Federation. They have arms and so they bring nothing but destruction. And let these territories be three times that of ancient Donbas, they are and will remain Ukrainian. So are all those who stand here – the avatars, the spineless rookies, the motivated fighters, the careless of lost opportunities or the crazed suits – everyone is here in order to stop them. To finally stop them. Once and for all. Also, maybe, a lot of people realize that not everything depends on us. And some, I am sure, don't realize anything, not even what their contribution to all this is.

This war is strange. At least the stage that it's at now. Seasoned troops explain that at the beginning of the war, in the total disorganization and the deadly mess, they could understand the goal – the freeing of the territory from the militants, the victory of good over evil. And here today's war doesn't have a goal. This is a Wall. A guard tower.

Further into the cold and wild. Mance Rayder and the White Walkers. On the other side are Westerns. And whoever rules there, whatever clandestine plots or games of thrones take place, their task and our task is to defend the wall.

Hardly any of the troops believe Donbas will ever be part of Ukraine again. Victory is an illusion. The IED that accidentally went off in the bush can disturb the whole platoon for an hour or maybe two. Chaotic shooting from the other side or from various positions confirms that this is an outright military offensive. Especially at night. That's why the news of the ceasefire is viewed with skepticism: not everyone has nerves of steel, and the arrangements in Minsk or Paris are like Plexiglas through which you can see only the contours of completely optimistic hopes. Here they are still laboring in the mines and no one is safeguarded from the stupid fire opened by the drunk.

The war will last as long as it takes to demine the last bush and for the checkpoints to grow over with wild grapes or young maples. But for now the soldiers of the Night Watch are standing against the wall and scanning the cold darkness. They have no expectation of anything. They aren't waiting for anything. Except maybe for the changing of the guard, a leave, or demobilization.

Neighbors

It's important to feel a connection to the area where you come from, to know that right beside you there is a person who has walked down the street where you grew up and who maybe even knows the teacher at your school and maybe even some of the people closest to you.

During war it's important to have someone from your area of the country. Even if he isn't from your specific city, even if you just lived for some time in the same city or in the same region.

Where am I from – Cherkasy or Kyiv? I lived in both cities for an equal amount of time. The roads leading from both cities intersect like the stitches on traditional Ukrainian embroidery, but both of them lead nowhere. Uncle Lyosha, an old wolf, hunched over by tempestuous years of pirating and shepherding in Altay, is from the Cherkasy region, but his city is more than 200 km from Cherkasy, the actual city. His town is twenty kilometers from the Vinnytsya region and twenty-five kilometers from the Kyiv region. To Kyiv it's one hundred and eighty kilometers. But Uncle Lyosha is my neighbor anyway. Uncle Lyosha is my only true compatriot. And for him I am the only true neighbor. He calls me jokingly in Russian "Artem, my neighbor."

In my platoon there are three guys from Kyiv. It seemed to me that they should absolutely be – my compatriots, companions, soul mates in this distant Luhansk region, a staunch brotherhood on enemy territory. But one of them was thrown out and terminated for deserting, another for alcoholism.

The third one serves well, even skillfully, if such a definition works at a neighboring defense point. They say that he is clever and crafty, frequents the hospitals all the time, petitioning the medical commissions, plotting something, and, of course, drinking.

Uncle Lyosha is with me, shoulder to shoulder, so to speak, from the time on the train that took us from Rivne to Haysyn. It's the old guy with blue tattoos on his fingers. We've been through everything together. We've argued, made up, drunk, eaten, been on duty together until morning. He is about sixty. He is an old man known in his circles. I'm also known in my circles. And these circles are, let's just say, particular in each of our cases.

When the old man is annoyed with me for some reason, instead of peacefully and politely calling me a neighbor, he disparagingly calls me a Kyivite. For him, as for a person with a difficult past, it's natural to identify people according to their geographical region: Kirovohrad, Cherkasy, Donetsk.

"So, one time, we the Cherkasy folks came to visit the Donetsk folks," he narrates.

I know these people from Cherkasy. When we were young, their names and criminal nicknames were known to all of us. Legends were created about them. The press wrote about these people in the early '90s. This time I eagerly listen to their stories which seem to be truthful, rather than just being myths and legends. But they are about the same legendary monarchs of the criminal world.

Uncle Lyosha is a witness to this brotherhood, a buddy I never had before. My life experiences allowed me to have enemies, friends, acquaintances, accomplices, colleagues, comrades, interlocutors, classmates, and groupmates, but never any compatriots, or neighbors. Compatriots only existed for me in Soviet movies and old village customs. Compatriots were a pretext for drinking. Compatriots are like distant extended family: brothers-in-law, sisters-in-law, and uncles. They have little to do with the modern cosmopolitan world or globalism. But if you think about it, war doesn't fit into the modern world well. A compatriot is an outdated concept, like war. Instead of creating, discovering, growing wheat, exploring space, or going to parties with drunk DJs, I sit in the middle of the steppe with a machine gun in my hands. With something that can kill people. It is something from the Middle Ages. I think that sometime in the future when historians study our present they will call it the Middle Ages. "God," they will say, appalled. "These people drank water from plastic, used gas, and killed one another with metal."

That's how I always thought about compatriots. These people didn't care for the open and honest, but for those that lived on the same street with them! But now I have Uncle Lyosha. My compatriot. And, more than that, he is a friend in the service. A brother-in-arms. A person who says what he thinks, has criminal inclinations, and tells jokes about homosexuals.

Donbas's Quiet Sun

A year ago I wanted to join the army. The desire had been bubbling up in me for a few months already. The worsening situation on the front, the deep connection with my country, the call to fulfill obligations. But the alarm clock rang at 7:30 a.m., and I got ready, got my son ready for daycare and thought: "Lord, I can stand anything but these morning wake-up calls. And also in the cold"... And in the army, and especially during war – it's extremely difficult. One moment I jump on the train, fifteen minutes later I'm sitting in the office, drinking coffee, and there it is dark, cold and scary, there is a war and uncertainty, some otherworldly fear and prehistoric carnage – metal against the people. There is capture, castration, and a lifetime of slavery in the mountains of Ichkeria. That is the potential fate of a soldier captured by the Russians. And for a time the desire to enlist in the army disappeared. Even though the call to fulfill an obligation, naturally, didn't disappear.

Now I get up at one o'clock. At five in the morning I leave. It's dark, cold, sometimes scary. And it's OK. It's a lot better than being in an office. There is also coffee here, considerately left by my brothers-in-arms. And there are weapons. And you can take a leak on any bush. And your group of boys are in touch with you via walkie-talkie... And here it is already dawning, and frost covers the earth – but it doesn't cover you, and you – you stare into the darkness and then back behind the bunker. You close your eyes and think about the eternal: family, achievements, sex... you even think about God once in a while. Well, you think. We all think about God. Sometimes. I don't like the banal lyrics that say that no one can remain an atheist while being shot at. Some days ago, a chaplain gave me a blessed medallion. More accurately, he gave me about thirty. Right at the twentieth outpost, across from the large, painted yellow-blue letters that spelled out the name "Popasna," they gave us some volunteer help. He led me aside and asked quietly.

"Do you have any bullets? Gimme several packets of seven sixty-twos."

"I don't have any," I answered. "I only have five forty-fives."

"Then here," and he poured a whole handful of medallions into my hand. "Give 'em to your boys."

And I put one of them around my neck. Instead of a bullet or a white plastic cross. Or not instead of, but just there. Not so that it protects you, but so that... But why not? And it is Catholic, I don't really know anything about this, but this medallion suddenly reminds me of Naples. And I sit at night in the cold in the middle of the steppe and I think about warm southern Italy and all those bronze, marble, and other decorative Virgin Marys on every corner and about how I took leave at my own cost, so that I could go there, and how for an entire week I didn't have to get up at my usual 7:30 a.m.

And so there – in other words, here – it turns out that it's not that bad. It's not always filled with death and also, miraculously, every morning above this gray zone the purple glow of the dawn rises. The sun. The quiet and redeeming sun of Donbas.

New Old Dream

I've been having the same dream for ten years. I have to go to school again – to finish classes there for another two or three years. This dream is troubling, chimerical: arguments about the fact that I already have a higher education, a family, a real life – don't work. I sit at the desk and try to figure out: how should I reconcile this academic life with real life, how can I stand being forced to sit behind a desk and how can I hide my shame when I look into my parents' eyes? I completed my studies a long time ago, but it turns out something didn't go right, I made a mistake at some point, maybe didn't pray to the right god or turned an envelope in to the wrong person, and because of that I didn't get a diploma. It's really a terrible dream. It makes me think that time is like a spider web that can be torn and pulled into a spiral, and it sucks you in, so that you emerge in the most unpleasant circumstances that you haven't lived through for a long time.

Today for the first time I dreamed about being discharged from the army. And even before I got all the required signatures on my discharge papers and turned in my weapons along with my helmet and machine gun, I got the news. I am being involuntarily retained in the army and this time I don't know how to tell my wife that we won't be going to Amsterdam. Or tell my son that the outing to the soccer match between "Dynamo" and "Barcelona" is canceled. And how do I tell my parents that I did serve out my entire year, honorably and faithfully on my surveillance posts, completely kept the un-written laws of army service, successfully avoided the enemy's bullets, ate at the prescribed time, and didn't crawl out of the bunker without my helmet?

And so, some meters away from garbage cans, on which "REU-4" is stenciled with white paint, my guys stand. Also with news. "And where are you going?" I ask them. And they – they know they aren't going with me. Someone is going to the third regiment, someone to the 79th brigade, some-one to the mountain infantry. And me? Where am I going? Once again, to the mechanized infantry. What will I do without you guys? I am standing near my home in Cherkasy, next to the boiler room, almost crying. In one hand I carry my news and in the other, a camping cooking pot and a machine gun. Should I turn them in or not? Or maybe turn them in, sign off, take new equipment, and sign off again.

It looks like it is not only our trip to Amsterdam and the outing to soccer that are canceled, but also my whole life. The training field again, the mess of the army, faces so familiar they make you want to throw up, the newly designed rules, commanders without any army experience, forms for "Can I go to the post office?" "What's in the bag?" "National Guard on checkpoints?" "formation," "widespread separatist mentality," abstaining from sex, showers, sleep, dry white wine with seafood, and some Parmesan on your tongue.

And then I hear:

"Artem! Artem! Sorry that I woke you up. The captain is asking to borrow the infrared camera..."

"Playdough, is that you?"

"Sure, my dear."

"Here is the infrared camera and batteries."

"Do you have cigarettes?"

"Here, have a pack. It's OK, take it. I have a carton. Are you leaving for the third regiment? No? Well, stop by for coffee in the morning."

We Succeeded

Everyone had their own reasons for standing on the Maidan. My best friend stood for bike paths. My other friends, for smoothies and cupcakes (I'm exaggerating, of course I'm exaggerating). Someone's business was taken away along with their freedom of choice. For sure, there were those who defended personal interests – at least some of those who distrust the West see the Maidan as the manifestation of the middle class and small business demands.

Well, I stood for a visa-free agreement with the EU. That was my current concern, due to my late initiation into the world of European tourism.

Here in the army I hardly ever met anyone who protested on the Maidan or anyone who supported a revolutionary path. Most people are for "stability," a popular election slogan of Yanukovych. Money is the true measurement of happiness. True corruption is preferable to liberal chaos. And for most of them, for us who took part, standing our ground and protesting, we were not successful. The result of our slogans "Out with the Mob" and "Ukraine is Europe!" were political collapse, war, and grandmothers who hung themselves over gas bills!

Smoothies and cupcakes? Here they laugh at this. How do I explain to a miner from Dnipropetrovsk or a beekeeper from Vinnytsya the importance of the availability of a mandarin smoothie and blueberry cupcakes in the wrapper, called Odwalla or something equally pretentious? That is ridiculous. It can't be understood. That is not why we occupied the Maidan.

Bike paths? Sinking into the mud and devouring expired canned goods, staring into the tumultuous and damp beyond, all we hope for is that nothing will land here from that milky distance. It's strange to think of bike paths and a new blue mountain bike. There is more hope that after the war I will still have legs to turn the pedals of the old "Ukraine" bike. Bike paths remain on the Greater Land, and the Greater Land exists only for the privileged.

Definitely not for us. At least not for now. And for most of the fighters all this is indistinguishable stupidity and craziness. And almost a perversion. "Yuck. There's nothing for people to eat." And you can't dispute it.

The question of a visa-less system is not a fundamentally interesting issue. A much more important issue is that of a one-sided cease-fire. By the way, we find out about most of our generals' orders from news broadcasts. Here I could argue, rave, and roar that the objective of the conflict – is not the object of the conflict. The Maidan happened for this reason, the prospect of a visa-less system woke up a lot of our people to the possibility of something wonderful, beautiful, it offered us a whiff of something fragrantly sublime. But there is also the argument: even on the Piazza del Popolo a pig will only forage for acorns. And the saying about the goat in the garden also applies here in my opinion. Also, how can there be a visa-less system when there are soldiers at the front?

Living in medieval conditions. The early Middle Ages. They say: "Soon I will be crushing fleas and spitting blood into my fists, and here you are talking about beauty and fragrance."

I agree. A lot of things here lose their meaning. Especially if a half a year ago you yourself were almost a hipster in the capital who dreamed of becoming famous like Rimbaud and handsome like Rambo. The very word "smoothie" evokes in you a condescending smile and the pretentious clothing of those who frequent the establishment, sardonic laughter. Well, at least Homeric. Your tasks today are to survive, to stay healthy, because a third of the soldiers belong in the hospital. Dampness, cold, alcohol, unhealthy (though tasty) food, and constant stress all promise us a merry waste of time in long hospital lines. Well, yes, I know, soldiers are needed to suffer through adversities and have the opportunity to defend their country. And then the soldiers don't give a damn about this decorative shit that makes the cities beautiful and the inhabitants of the cities happy. They don't give a damn until they go on vacation. Let's say they go to the capital. For about two weeks. And if in the first days you remain an old soldier, who doesn't know how to express love, at the end of the stay in the big city you will soften, your soul will melt, and in your head a strange thought will appear: maybe I should go to a smoothie bar.

Oh yes, that's what it is. Certainly, because you are drowning here in mud, soot, and diesel, you are sharing the shelter of the bunker with small rodents, sleeping with open eyes and believing in future happiness. With the clear conscience of a citizen of a country that beat corruption, you'll be able to ride on a new blue mountain bike straight to Europe.

A Unique Fall

This fall is unique in my life. Maybe I should write something special about this fall. Something in the spirit of Robert Frost. It's not about the war, but about the earth. It's a story about *chornozem*, rich soil. Or about a soldier's feet. Or about mice. About their deaths. Mice die in many ways, fall dead on your head, dry up in our sack, burn up in the stoves, choke from eating their fill of brand-name sweets.

You could write about it or even better sing a psalm about a soldier's feet and field mice. With a choir. Solemnly accompanied by a harpsichord. This would be an overblown illustration of the conditions of living in the unit. And in this story there would be chapters "wet wood," "the sound of silence," and even "washed hands." And not one word about war, weapons, or war technology.

A kind of field absurdity, a forest grotesque, underground buffoonery. And all this would be unwaveringly performed by a choir of sergeants. And when it came to the part about the death of mice, the sergeants, would stomp their feet. A soldier's feet.

By the way, we have a battle flag, the flag that made it through Savur-Mo-hyla, a strategic height near Donetsk that our troops fought for; the flag that experienced a heavy battle below Marynivka, that flag was injured, got a contusion, but is terrified of mice. It slept on the street, until they brought us a whole box of "death". A mouse's death. Small bags like tea bags, with turquoise pills inside. They don't make you die right away. First a paroxysm occurs, blood pressure rises, then craziness, madness, and then death. Ugly and painful as it usually happens during war. Death from turquoise, from bodies that sweat in damp underground quarters, from love for Ukrainian soldiers, and from the desire not to have to go into the fields to look for seeds: the harvest didn't take place because of the fierce tank battle below the city of Popasna. And the sergeants would serenade the dead mice, would stomp their yellow cracked heels on the black cracked *chornozem*. And the scent of sour borscht would waft over enemy positions, and the bravura of the whistling "Cossacks" would catch the attention of our monitors. And the mice… those that survive, would go to the southern limits, close to Pervomaisk, the Orthodox camps, surrounded by the Ukrainian defense points.

And when this unique autumn ends, when the *chornozem* freezes, then soldiers will pull on their woolen socks. That's when we will burn birch wood in the stoves, hang New Year's garlands on the clay walls of the bunkers and lift our glasses to our comrade, Otaman Driomov, a separatist military leader caught up in the war against his own, so that he may rest in peace, even if he is still alive. And the sweet-voiced sergeants will stand on the perimeter of the main field that separates us from them, and start singing. Solemnly and loudly, as if for the last time. Confidently breaking the ice of frozen puddles with their feet. This fall I will remember forever and until the end of my life, I'll carry it in my heart. Like something extremely intimate. And I will remember it only in moments of happiness. As truly exceptional and genuine.

Almost like in the Stories

Valyusha, the louse, sitting at the third line of defense, calling his wife and rambling on about how he picked up the entrails of his friends – my commander screams in anguish, telling the story of his close neighbor.

There are so many of those stories. Even during training there were similar stories that were told to friends or family at night, informing them about the fierce fights and endless bombardments.

"Why am I drunk? Sweetie, why wouldn't I get drunk here? At night I dragged Styopa, who had a head wound, through an enemy outpost." Sweetie bursts into tears, sits down, her hair turning gray. The spicy scent of Corvalol, a heart medication, in a benign plume, reaches all the way to the staircase. The neighbors try to comfort her. They don't say anything to the children. Just so that he comes back alive. Even without hands, even without legs, but alive. Our Kolinka. Our defender.

The defender runs to the closest village for additional supplies. Styopa waits at the checkpoint. After two days of deprivation, everything is falling apart. Will you lend me fifty kopecks until the fifteenth? I'll give it back, I promise. Another has been burning wagons and civilian wheelbarrows for two months near Izum. He got lucky – he lives in the café, at the outpost there is an oven. Cigarettes, drinks, constant amounts of money flow into his pockets. Yes, it isn't as safe as the National Guard, but you can live. It's just sad somehow. Sadness poisons the soul. At home, in dear Starkon, Natasha waits. He calls her, crying: "Yesterday they demolished part of the platoon, showered it with bullets. A sniper. Am I wounded? Yes, but no. I have a contusion. Two contusions. I love you, pray for us. Oh, and send me some sausages. Kisses."

My friend the beekeeper Sanya B. only told his sisters where he is. His mother believes that he is still studying on a training base in Mykolaiv.

Why should I worry her? After three months – demobilization, then I will tell everyone. We'll laugh about it.

Old Kolya with the nickname "Rifleman" is already fighting a second year. He survived the Debaltsevo encirclement. He saw more than any psychological resources can tolerate. Sometimes he falls apart, drinks, and cries. His parents think he is in Kharkiv making money.

Even without knowing, his mom has turned all gray and his old man has a bad heart. Some go out to check the neighboring outpost every one hundred meters and before that they make sure they have signed their wills, calling all their acquaintances, describing their adventures, and highlighting their heroic successes. Others take part in dangerous engagements, capturing trophy armored cars, then crawling for hours over mine fields and lying in wait and then telling their friends and family about the monotony of staying in their positions. "Shooting?" "Nobody is trying to get us." Everything is quiet here. Like in a tank.

"She died," my commander said.

"Who?" I didn't understand.

"Remember I told you about that louse Valya, who is stationed near Lisichaskyi and calls his wife everyday and tells her horror stories. To make a long story short, Valya called, talked a ton and after ten minutes – that's it, her heart couldn't take it. They could not bring her back to life. Two kids. Almost like in that story."

"Which story?"

"I don't remember."

11120th Day of Life

I slept through the last month and a half of 2008. We slept through it. My wife and I together. We went to bed at 10 p.m. and we woke up close to lunch. The financial crisis was still at its height, money was running out, and we didn't have the motivation to work. We were sucked in by lethargy, we had almost zero will to live. I remember that one night we decided to try something new. In the end, we lost forty dollars at the casino. It wasn't only our way of life we had to change, but also our environment and surroundings. So we decided to move to the village. All of this wasn't about forty dollars, of course, but for other reasons like frustration, feeling trapped, being disoriented, and exhaustion.

Today I feel something similar. A complete absence of any desire to do anything, to want anything, to dream. Yesterday morning when we all woke up, it suddenly struck me that the thing that bothers me most is the lack of windows. Just being able to wake up and look out a window. At the trees, the birds, the dark water and thick fog, to look at the wet asphalt and the advertisements on the corner, at the umbrellas and children. At the homeless even. But here in order to see daylight, you need to get dressed and crawl outside into frost, wind, and fog.

In the bunker, it's light and warm. Even hot. Vlad heats it up so much; it's as if he has childhood trauma related to being cold. We drip with sweat, we are annoyed by flies. Yesterday someone came back drunk and spilled condensed milk on the table. Now the sleeping bags, bunks, bags are sticky and sweet. The mice have become so brave that they sleep in our jacket pockets. They have their own lives here. Food, fun, sex, death. A few days ago I found three dead ones beneath the pillow. Rotten, stinking, mummified.

I hope that on December 19 St. Nick, a good saint who brings presents and puts them in your boots or under your pillow, will bring us something more than what we already have. Maybe he won't bring us anything at all. I don't want anything. Not even world peace, because then our presence here wouldn't make any sense. But we would have sat here anyway, and I would have written about snow and dirt, about blood and death, about sex and grease, about love and fuel. About alcohol and slag heaps. About weapons and the composition of our feces. About morning, about evening, again about morning and again about evening and then about night.

How did the night pass?

We were shooting. In the field, in the snow, in the sky, at the trees and at the enemy. They say someone was killed. They found a hat (Persian lamb with a pointed red top and a white cross) and a lot of blood on the snow.

In the evening (it starts to get dark here at 4 p.m.) nothing is visible, but the darkness is not scary. Even in the villages I have never experienced this. Walking from the guard post in the middle of the night, it feels like you're floating in the thick darkness.

The darkness is so thick. The generator roars, water runs, some figures in some station behind us light the sky with lanterns. Somewhere there is a bang, someone is arguing, neighbors are in the swamp up to the ribs and are chopping wood. Further in the distance, nothing is visible. But you don't need to see further anyway. The most important thing is for someone not to fire their gun while drunk. And on the other side are signal missiles again. They say that on such a night you can't expect anything. We sit, we wait. Leonidovych, a new sergeant, entered. He brought sausages, treated himself to some pastries, updated us on the newest rumors and news, complained about the commanders, promised new promotions, asked us to sign the orders, invited us to get wood in the morning.

We said no.

And somewhere out there, about ten kilometers from us, the war ended a long time ago. For the most part. War is not interesting...

I would like to sleep until January. Or to be awake, but preferably not here.

The 75th day on the front.

The 203rd day in the army.

The 11120th day of life.

A Miracle Didn't Happen

Everyone who was on the first line of defense confirms that one of the most common phobias among the soldiers – is to be killed in their bunkers. There are a lot of ways this could happen. By Chechens, coming to stab soldiers as they sleep, or by grenades which are hurled into the dugouts. We have it too. I sense it – this fear.

Almost every evening, falling asleep, I think: and will this night be the last? For some reason it isn't humane – to die defenseless, that way, in underpants and undershirt, dreaming about the Greater Land, not having the ability to fight back, because you won't take your machine gun to bed every night. Though I confess that it has happened. Especially when alone in the bunker. Of course, we always keep one or two knives beneath our pillows. Just in case.

This story was told to me by fighters in our battalion, who were demobilized back in August. It was December 2014 when they were in position between Volnovakha and Mariupol. Their main objective was to defend the bridge there, because a ton of explosives were stored under it. To make a long story short, they had to defend that bridge or blow it up. And then on that St. Nick's night, while some were standing watch at their posts and others were resting in their dugouts, one soldier, whose wife had baked gingerbread for the whole platoon, decided to walk through the bunkers and put a St. Nick's treat beneath everyone's pillow. The sentimental gesture almost resulted in mortal combat. It's not hard to understand how our own soldiers could almost have knifed him to death because of their fear.

It happens like this sometimes: an officer responsible for building morale, decides to find you in your bunker at three in the morning to tell you some very important news. As a warning: "Who's there, bastard? I'm gonna shoot!" – no reaction. It sometimes happened that they shot. So, all right, into the wall, as a warning. For some reason I naively decided that our education officer would visit all the bunkers with packages that evening. Well, why not? In the last ten years, St. Nick has never failed to leave me something (this expectation might be associated with ten years of family life?) And so, what now – is the war supposed to erase all that? No, I didn't sign up for this. At night I woke up several times, reaching under my pillow, expecting to finally feel something there. "Maybe," I thought. Vlad or Sanya will think of putting chocolate under there. And then I thought: And what about me? Did I think of it? Did I have something in for them? No? Forget it, soldier.

This year St. Nick passed me by, like big rivers pass by mountains. He just didn't get to the front. Maybe he was pissed. I'm even sure of it. Who wants to go visit godforsaken lands to visit godforsaken people? Why should he risk it? Who would pay him to take it? I wouldn't go either. Ukraine, Syria, Afghanistan, South Sudan. Never in my life. If I'm getting everything straight, St. Nick never promised anybody anything. Something that you can't just put beneath a pillow: understanding, justice, intelligence (this is from Sanya B.) and iron chrome dumbbells that weigh thirty-six kilograms.

New Year's Eve

They say that several vans of volunteers came to the headquarters with New Year's paraphernalia. Cookies, candy, some nice surprises, and even booze: someone said that they saw some brandy. All of this – for the boys, for those who must celebrate the New Year in their bunkers, far from their families. For our heroes. Our boys. Our stars.

But the only things that boys and heroes got were a box of mandarin oranges, a box of cookies, and a couple of pine branches. One of them we hung from the ceiling. Yura told us that mice are afraid of the scent of pine. He tricked us.

Preparations for holidays are the same there as they are here. In other words, they are the same here as they are there. On the morning of the 29th, Vlad and I accompanied Sanya on his leave and rushed to the center of Popasna where we got two bottles of champagne, ingredients for salads, and a bunch of other small things.

From home I received some red caviar, sausage, and a bottle of good alcohol. We drank the champagne right away as if we missed the bubbles, so the next day Vlad had to go to the city again.

On the 31st at 6 a.m. there was supposed to be some training, some kind of shooting, tank exercises in the surrounding villages. All this took place for writing off fuel consumption and, of course, it smelled of criminal activity. Vlad and I woke up, Leonidovych left us at home. In other words, in the "bunker." For our exemplary behavior, I think. At 8 a.m. we had already watched "Forrest Gump". We took baths, slept a little, shot into the echoing of the evening quiet just for fun. At lunch we drank the bottle of good alcohol.

Later in the afternoon we invited Uncle Lyosha. We drank again. Then there were fireworks, no worse than the ones in the city. Tracers and illuminated missiles flew into the New Year's sky from our side and from the opposing side. When our buccaneers, filled with frantic exaltation, set out in tanks to greet the separatists, I tumbled into bed. But I woke up a few times because wandering neighbors came to the bunker and invited us to join them, apologized for something, drank, helped themselves to chocolates and oranges, sang, talked a long time about nothing, forgot their scarves and phone cases, jumped outside, emptied a few rounds, loaded a hundred more, and ran further, into the darkness, into the frost, into the black holes, that transported them from one place to another – from one bunker to another – greeted their friends, drank liquor together (I think that at 3 a.m. there was only rubbing alcohol left); and again they set off firecrackers and flares, they fell into the snow, they made snow angels and thanked God that they were still alive, happy, and drunk.

In the morning the cold air woke me up (someone didn't cover the entrance with a blanket), in a mug I noticed leftover champagne – it smelled the same it did when I was a child. Stale champagne smells of happiness, gifts, leftovers from the New Year's feast, and the old Soviet cartoons. I got dressed quickly, took my gun, and wandered out to relieve the boys on duty. Near the bathroom there was a fight. It seems there was a new cook...

Responsibility

Sometimes I think I know how to fight. I know what to do, where and how to stand my ground, where to go if retreating is necessary to save lives, what I need to work on, and, mainly, what I need to improve on to make myself more disciplined. Sometimes it seems to me that I could lead the defense point. I could become an officer responsible for building morale or even a platoon commander. Some analytical know-how, some educational talks, a sense of humor, and of course, experience. But this is just what it seems like to me. Sometimes. In reality, leading is a thankless job. Just like any job with responsibilities. The army is full of bureaucracy. The chain of command, though crumbly like cookies in dried army rations, still exists. You shouldn't take too much on – you will end up at the bottom. You don't owe anyone anything; especially if you're a commander, an HR officer or mobilized official. For them the paperwork and the maintenance of the chain of command is of utmost importance. Experience has shown that going over rank and proper authorities in order to reach a goal (leave, adequate weapons, commendations, changes in orders or the solution to any other problem) is the wrong choice. Of course, it is inappropriate, bordering on a scandal, but otherwise you don't get anywhere. And given that I am a simple soldier, if a request comes from me, then the appropriate authority demands clear observance of all rules, the filling out of forms, adherence to all regulations, and obtaining the requirement permissions. And then at the meeting they make you beg like a dog. Naturally, this is painful and humiliating. "And what did you expect, stupid, aren't you the one responsible?"

I remember the men seriously urging me to transfer into the morale unit.

You have a degree, you are smart, you'll be a second lieutenant, and then first. Come on, man!

No, thank you. First of all, no one would seriously consider my candidacy, and second of all, I wouldn't succeed in complying with, let's call it, the red tape. Also, I'd make enemies from those with whom yesterday I ate meat from the same can. I'd go running into the bunkers, quieting the rowdy ones. I would make excuses before battle, ashamed to look them in the eye. I would know the names of all the military police who harass soldiers. I would try to release my fellows from the clutches of those enforcers, and towards the end I would lose all the documents that my guys turned in for getting the certificates of the participants of military operations, a set of documents that guarantee your social benefits later in civilian life.

No, thank you.

You sure?

I'm a seasoned soldier, my place is with my automatic rifle and thermal imager at the watch post. Responsibility is a scary thing. Our former platoon leader, "Maestro," kept commanding in the midst of a heart attack. Our supply man had it so hard that he is still recuperating. Leonidovych, our current commander, has lost some fifty pounds. And every time that it seems to me that I know how to fight, I come to the realization that I'm just a coward who is simply afraid of responsibility. Responsibility for my choices, for my personal circumstances. I recognize that it's easier to be an ordinary soldier, and I thank God that I'm not an officer. I thank the universe that I'm not part of the high command. My maximum would be as the commander of the division. And now, somehow, I find myself looking at officers in a different way. Sometimes I just feel sorry for them. I sympathize. I even sympathize with the corrupt ones who either wind up going to their new dacha or prison, because even so, they experience tremendous trauma and must endure a lot. In truth, I don't know how to conduct a war. How to run a country. Or how to fix the wiring in a light fixture.

Below Zero

For a month and a half, we experienced negative temperatures. It was all because of the swamp beneath our feet. Sometimes when you'd walk from the bunker to the kitchen or to the watch post, you'd drag pounds of mud with you, you'd curse the whole world, the war, your fate, this damn *chornozem*. The earth here is greasy, like army stew, the clay – tacky like kneaded dough. It sticks not only to your shoes, but also your clothes, hands, hair. You look at an army truck and are amazed by the fact that it is able to drive. If only we had one.

Towards the end of December freezing temperatures hit us. Life had become routine, movement quickened, logistics became more organized. But the temperature fell to minus twenty; not that we didn't anticipate it, of course, we did, but we dreaded it anyway. I think that's the way they wait for floods every year in Transcarpathia. Last winter, when I traveled over asphalt or on city transportation, when I slept somewhere soft and drank kefir and ate a grapefruit every day, I couldn't even imagine how the soldiers on the front were living, how they lived in minus fifteen temperatures. How did they wash themselves, go to the bathroom, wash their clothes?

Do they get sick, poor guys, do they try to keep their fingers from frostbite, standing at their posts or lying in wait. "I couldn't handle it," I thought, carefully peeling a grapefruit, so that the juice didn't get inside the cuts on my fingers. It turns out I could. That is, I can. And I even feel fine. At some point someone complained to me about my dissatisfaction with Rivne's educational system, they said: "Son, you've never had to shit in minus seventeen degree cold in the middle of a field. If you can shit normally, you can live." For the time being all the food has frozen, water turned to ice, the air – into something hard and stinging, and chopping wood – well, that has turned into a typical army version of a sport. Speaking of wood. It seems there was only one delivery from headquarters. At the beginning of October. I haven't seen such generosity from headquarters since. Chainsaws and saws, of course, are ours, bought with volunteer money, axes – too. Donbas forests are mercilessly cut, saws create sparks; because the trunks of trees are abundantly cut by bullets and shelling. To be able to wash up? The last time was last year. But they say this hardens you. It fortifies your soul, as they say, it strengthens your inner defenses.

Maybe it's true, but I always have a few packages of wet wipes with me just in case, to hell with my integrity. I'm on active duty. Four hours on watch during the day, how much at night – not as long as it seems. Of course, when it's minus five – minus ten, it's easier to suffer through it, but who will if not us, the recruits? The clothing – quilted (oh, our people can really sew for two bottles of precious vodka), felt boots, winter army pants, fall coats (our "Banner Leader" has a cool chic black coat, in which it isn't shameful to walk down a main street in some city like some Haysyn), down coats, and quilted jackets. Army outerwear is suited for early fall. At minus ten it's guaranteed that there will be an inflammation of some vital inner organ. Same thing for army boots that are only suitable for asphalt.

Dry asphalt, that is. And here, at the outpost, everything that is warm is fashionable even if it's not comfortable. Holding a weapon is clumsy, yes. I forgot that shooting is forbidden. So, you know, sit next to the stove, look into the crackling night, keep watch and hope that time will pass slowly, but it flies. What's worse, the weather forecasters promise it will go up to five degrees in several days in the Popasnianski district. And we have already experienced that ordeal. They say ordeals make us stronger.

Cerebral Palsy

Dima the medic, nicknamed Bones, brought her to us.

"You want me to bring you a cat? Everyone has a pet in their bunker, but you only have mice. I found her under the baths."

"Bring her!" we rejoiced.

And he did. A kitten. Tiny, black and white, very cute. A total cutie-pie that you can keep purring in your sleeping bag during cold Donbas nights.

But for some reason she was shaking. "She's just cold," the medic explained. "She'll warm up." Several days passed, but the kitten was still shaking. Even more. She couldn't walk and kept falling to the side, as if somebody had broken her spine. We thought that someone had stepped on her or sat on her, or someone kicked her after she appeared suddenly at their feet. Or maybe Bones hurt her while getting her out from under the sinks.

The first days she was sitting near the stove, warming herself, getting used to the new conditions. She hardly crawled out from her hiding place, and wasn't eating. But then, we fed her with what we were eating: canned fish, sardines, lentils with canned meat, vacuum packed foods.

A week passed, maybe even two. The kitten would crawl out to the surface more often. When nobody was in the bunker, she bravely ran all over our sleeping bags (leaving dirty paw prints), ate, and, of course, slept a lot. But she still was not walking normally. She mostly crawled, kind of. And kept shaking.

We called her Cerebral Palsy. And for some reason we could not love her. We did try hard to squeeze out the love of a big soldier for a tiny kitten, we took care of her, we even petted her, but it still didn't matter. At best, we felt a tiny bit of compassion mixed with annoyance. We were very pissed that she walked on our bedding, shat wherever she pleased, and totally refused to go outside.

Sometimes we forgot to feed her, and she meowed in an off-putting way. We stopped paying attention to her and in general treated her like we would treat a paralyzed relative toward whom we felt no emotions but a sense of responsibility. All there was left to do was give them sponge baths, feed them, and let the sound of their voice irritate us.

For the holidays we decided to spoil the kitten. We bought her a pack of cat food, a goulash made from three kinds of meat. From this treat, poor Cerebral Palsy puked all over Sanya's mattress. Then she started pissing on our sleeping bags and pillows. And our relationship with her fell apart completely.

The end came with the deluge. I mean the episode from our life in the dugout, when for forty-eight hours snow seemed to fall in ready piles, and on the third day the temperature rose unexpectedly, and we woke up from water falling into our ears. It totally flooded the stairs of the bunker. My sneakers were rocking on the water like paper boats in the March streams. Our stash of toilet paper was soaked. Only the bottom part of my mattress turned out to be dry.

Of course, Cerebral Palsy had no place to go, and so gave us an offended look, as if we specifically orchestrated this deluge to cause her discomfort. I think these were the kinds of thoughts that went through her head.

Of course, we dried out the bunker. And made new stairs. And cleaned the space behind the stove where the cat made her bed. We even got her a box and put rags in it. We tried to explain to her that these are natural disasters, and we suffer from them as much as the next person. But the kitten didn't stop pissing on the sleeping bags, shaking, and continually irritating us with her presence.

Then Hound, a machine gunner from our company, offered to adopt her.

"Isn't she cute," he said.

We sighed with relief. As if the paralyzed relative was taken to hospice. Things might have turned out differently, had we loved her.

Boys

The locals call us "boys." We are all "boys" in their eyes. I don't know what they call us in their private kitchens – cartels, robbers, pirates, invaders, liberators, armed forces, combatants, ATOs, heroes, westerners, these same ones, those same ones, simply military and soldiers, maybe even young soldiers, but to our face they all call us "boys."

"Boys, have some water."

"So there the boys stood, saw everything."

"Come on, boys, help me with the stroller."

They come up to us in a businesslike way and ask for money, and they also always ask, "When will it all end?" Loudly they remind us about our "parents and kids who are waiting at home." And they lecture us about something from their high and mighty Donbas point of view. In these circumstances the word "boys" is neutral, not yours, not theirs, in it there is something Cossack or Kuban. As if "boys" is a Ukrainian word in essence even when it is pronounced with a Russian accent. This is how Russians cite Ukrainian songs or proverbs, "bridle those horses, boys" or "when granny gets off the wagon the horse's load is lighter." And they typically use the same word when talking about those who are fighting on the other side. "Well, when the boys on the 14th of June were here" or "And the boys from Pervomaisk are freezing just like you?"

All of us – the Armed Forces of Ukraine and the separatists – we're all the same to them. Right now, we are here, and so we are – their bread, their sausage, and their made-in-Turkey jeans. No tenderness, sympathy, or gratitude – only pragmatism, only business. We aren't bad off and we leave a considerable amount of money in their stores and cafés, we pay for rides in their taxis, we leave tips at the local market. One taxi driver told us that today he makes two times more than before the war. Pizza parlors and coffee shops serve soldiers from morning to night without a break and the soldiers leave generous tips. There are hardly ever conflicts, and if there are, then they are usually between the socially unstable ones of the local front. It's changed into a provincial place where tourists go in their free time – to see the same church and to be in the same canyon. A new post office, an old post office, the loud sounds of the train station, the branches of banks, the delivery of humanitarian aid, acquaintances in the commander's office, friendly National guards on duty, trips to Artemivsk, and of course, soldiers – it seems that they were always there. It's just that here instead of coffee shops we have army headquarters. The price of apartments in the suburb of Cheryomushka dropped and at night, you can hear how some of the boys shoot at the other ones.

One popular restaurant where a lot of soldiers eat has the Wi-Fi password "crimeaisours." And for several months we were trying to figure out the owner's sympathies, what meaning did they imbue in this password, what cultural, historical, and psychological code is hidden in these Latin letters? Whose is Crimea? "Ours," Ukrainian or "ours," Russian? If we consider the fact that most of her clients were soldiers, and she was always warm and smiling, it be likely that she was on our side, and that "crimeaisours" was nothing more than some creative patriotic word play.

On the other hand, couldn't this be evil trolling or a totally hardened position, invincible, and stoic? Like that of the separatists. Anyway, somehow we provoked her and she became hostile. It seemed that she was suffering from some unresolved mental conflict.

"Boys," she yelled, "Listen to me, I am a Crimean, I am for Crimea. And it will always be ours. While you're lounging around here, the separatists are digging more trenches. Crimea is Russian. Kyiv is Russian. And who are you? It would be better if you defended us." Her unwavering use of boys didn't annoy me as much as it outraged me. And I couldn't do anything about it. I got used to it. We are all "boys" to them. I'm a "boy" for the taxi drivers whose convictions are hidden deeper than the pharmacists' or firefighter's. I'm a "boy" for the post office clerks who should have already gotten used to the fact that we, these "cartel boys," are regular guys, simple, naive, and kind. And I am a "boy" for the women in the market, who cannot get over their surprise at the military presence, as if war is something that belongs in the distant past, and we – we are something along the lines of a Soviet military force occupying Germany.

We went with Vlad to the post office and on the way we met an old woman. Very old, in a gray tattered scarf, pulling a sled with some discarded Christmas trees on it. She stopped us and said quietly and sincerely, in Ukrainian, unlike the others we meet in this city:"Dear boys, thank you. Thank you for being here. I am picking up the trees, taking them home – we don't have any wood. Thank you, dear boys."

Two Years Ago

Two years ago I also stood at an outpost, I'm talking about the Maidan. I was among those who reinforced the barricades with batons. It's true that back then I could go home any time. Eventually, late at night, I did just that. Tires burned, park benches cracked, enveloped by flames, men were everywhere, a lot of men. They were typical Maidan participants, for which occupying Hrushevskyi Street in Kyiv is the first phase of protest, and the night before December 17th is just a typical event in the protest, for which they, of course, were ready. They knew what to do and they did it. Calm and collected. Their war was still before them. Tomorrow there would be the expected battle and the first blood bath in the very center of the capital. Some of them won't return. In the midst of the calm and collected men were hysterical ones, frantically running. "We will all die!" they yelled.

We will all die sooner or later. Someone will depart behind these barricades. Sooner or later. Stepping aside from their shaky positions, they will put on yellow ski glasses that are bulletproof and they will attack. And there, hiding behind a lamp post and enveloped by the humid gray sky, they will give their soul to God. It was cold and humid that day. A short, determined old man ran up to us.

"Hey, guys, there are six benches over there, you need to bring them here."

He nervously pulled at his mustache and with his hand in gloves with exposed fingers he pointed to the place where the benches stood. We carried them closer with three other boys. And then with numb fingers we dug up some concrete, put it into bags, and moved them closer to the first barricade right across from the border of Independence. And then I stood and drank tea. Drank tea and watched the Trade Union Building burning.

Just like now. I'm just standing, drinking tea, and staring at familiar landscapes. A bush, the greenery, one more bush…

Who is covering me on the left?

This is one calling two! One calling two! I say hoarsely into my walkie-talkie.

One is online.

"Berlusconi." Are you on again?

I'm on only so I can warm up.

Over and out.

It's clear. No one is covering me on the left.

Today I am on watch alone. In fact, I'm the only one in our whole platoon, in other words I am responsible for the lives of seventy soldiers on my watch. And so I have to cover the whole left side of the bush myself as well as the right. But I know every branch and bend. If I look through the night vision or infrared scope from a certain angle, then the branches of the trees create the word "Chekh." I noticed this in October. When I could still think and analyze. When I still could be surprised. When I didn't believe in reality or trust my peaceful surroundings. It was deceptive and insidious like a foggy night. It is now balanced and empty. Of course, those who cross the desert in caravans must feel this way. A quiet danger, a distant road, absolute self-control.

For a long time now, I'm not thinking and analyzing. Yes, I stand and observe. The field, bush, the field, bush… Almost like it was two years ago.

This is one calling two. One calling two. One, fuck, pick up the transceiver.

This is one.

Are you sleeping?

I'm sleeping but I hear everything.

War Isn't Fashionable

It is easy not to notice war. No matter how paradoxical this sounds. If the war doesn't exist in the traditional context that we are used to. If our cities aren't bombed, our women aren't raped, our children don't go into the forest as partisans. So then the war isn't real to us. It's taking place somewhere else, not where we are. Most of us, that is.

But not all. We (soldiers, of course) talk about this a lot. Usually expressively and categorically, adding curses to our conversations, jargon, and slang. For us war didn't become just a distinct period in our lives, it became a pivotal stage in our lives. We haven't avoided it even though that could have happened.

We don't know if we'll make it to demobilization and if not, how exactly we will leave this world: crapping our pants with fear, or buried up to our ears in the ground, or being heroes with noble shot-through chests? And maybe killed by friendly fire? Or we will die accidentally, having handled a weapon carelessly? But for as long as we are alive, we'll talk about the war openly and honestly, using cursing creatively.

When will this war end? How? Who will write the pact about surrender? Whose efforts will be rewarded? Who will get reparations? Who is the first one who will be hung on the lamp posts near the opera theater? We talk about this happily and blatantly. We honestly admit in the most frightening situations that war will never end. It will either stop or it will grow into something more frightening, monstrous, and without compromise. Decades would have to pass for these wounds to heal. How soon will the war end? In a year, or two, or five. But it will live for a long time in the souls of its witnesses. This isn't an anti-terrorist operation with a happy ending but a serious conflict with borders, military forces, politics, with a civilian population that supports each of the sides. There are occupiers, collaborators, businessmen, diplomats; betrayal, duplicity, and victory. There are captives (not hostages as the press likes to call them sometimes).

There are still commanders. Do they also play their own games? Some transport Popasna pine trees out to their summer cottages on the only working ambulance, leaving the medics with a damaged Gazelle. Others play at being a patriot or the father of the nation, making tearful speeches, but in reality, hating all mobilization efforts. And there are those that foolishly signed a new contract while the "Anti-Terrorist Operation" was still in effect ("we believe this operation will be over in two weeks.") They are all, for us, a subject of uncensored language, jargon, and slang. And in my experience, I haven't met a soldier who didn't succumb to disappointment, and total distrust of the government.

We all witnessed how easy it is to make money from this war, how the enemy encourages writing off stolen goods, how rivers of fuel flow, how excuses about the lack of resources come from the commander's mouth, how those that take soldiers over the separating line are protected, with what enthusiasm some officers facilitate the travel of "contraband" to the other side. We see this war the way it is. And we see ourselves the way we are.

Disheartened, wind-blown, scorched, coarse, usually apathetic with sick eyes, inflamed gums, and extreme in opinions. Changeable and chaotic. Somewhere there, on the Greater earth, the war stopped existing. The war stopped being fashionable. Patriotism faded a long time ago like last week's perfume, then maybe it turned into commerce. It seems that only the president speaks about patriotism. Everyone else is quiet. They don't even pay last respects to the fallen soldiers. Dying is also unfashionable. Especially during war.

They Don't Like
Those Kind in the Army

They don't like people like me in the army. I ask too many questions. I get upset, I value integrity, and also, I lack initiative; I can't help analyzing the command's orders and the illogical nature of their behavior in their own units. People like me won't ever sign an enlistment contract. I think I am in the army by accident. Not in the war, but in the army. The war should be the concern of every citizen who cares about his country. The army is a separate institution, which, unfortunately, is unquestionably tied to war. But it would be better if young entrepreneurs could be in charge of war. Some entrepreneurs who know how to work towards a goal, who could analyze a situation critically and come up with unusual methods to conduct the war. War – well, war is a creative endeavor, not a well-known pathway where bureaucratic concerns are more important than people's lives. It's difficult to achieve results, no matter who you are, when there is nothing in your office but a stapler and a calculator.

It's impossible to achieve results if no one is setting any goals, other than how to organize a desk, caulk windows, or sort green and yellow paper clips. Though I have to give credit where credit is due: the new salary of seven thousand hryvnias makes a lot of people want to enlist in the army. Especially those who in their civilian lives don't make more than two grand. And if we add those already serving, it comes out to a sizable amount even by the capital's standards. You might even think about quitting drinking. You could obtain a rank, a position, a raise in salary. It encourages. Inspires. Motivates. This conflict in the east will drag on for a long time and with every wave of mobilization, the quality of the army's new recruits goes down just like the level of morale.

This last year of the war showed that this situation creates serious difficulties. Most of those mobilized, who are sitting in swamps and positions in the sunburnt prairies of Donbas and salt marshes of Crimea, don't entirely understand the goal. If it is to free Donbas, then give the command; if it is to sit and rot in the bunkers, then pay us more; and if you happen to know what it is, then at least tell us why we are here. The problem with motivation is the fault of the commanders, who seldom communicate with those under their command, don't understand their problems, and if they do, they deliberately ignore them. "That's the way the army is," some say. "We are a poor country that is fighting." "In many companies it is even worse," others say. And it really is worse. The guys from the neighboring battalion say that in their three months on the front drinking water hasn't ever been delivered to them, and as for luxuries like cheese or sausage (which, we can say, our battalion isn't deprived of), they know them only as utopian dreams. And so they sit, chew dried army rations, and stand on guard duty. Every time I hear them being attacked, I think that cheese, sausage, and drinking water would make their lot just a little better.

I was mobilized. Not enslaved, but mobilized. I can assert my rights, express my opinions, argue with my commanders, or express my opposition without any thought about the consequences. A soldier who voluntarily enlists wouldn't be able to do that, whatever infraction he commits would lead to dire consequences. And I know from my own experience in arguing with administrators in every job I had that I'd never sign an enlistment contract. The ability to keep quiet is the most useful habit in the army. The ability to follow an order without asking questions is of utmost value. Obedience and zeal are the keys to a successful career. Just as they probably are at any government job where the only innovation that occurred was the installation of metal and vinyl replacement windows.

I don't know, maybe somewhere there are places where bureaucracy and duplicity in accounting are unacceptable, and where soldiers are valued not because they don't drink but because of their professional military abilities. Maybe there are places where there is a leader in the service, who on seeing a soldier sawing oak logs that are forty centimeters in diameter with a hand saw feels something close to shame. Maybe there are places where soldiers are given yogurt and fruit for breakfast. I don't know. But I know for sure that I'll never sign an enlistment contract because they don't like those like me in the army.

A Unique Winter

This winter has been a unique one in my life. Maybe it's worth writing a little about it. Maybe something in the style of Varlam Shalamov and Isaac Babel. The first one wrote accounts of the Gulag, the second about the Polish-Soviet War of 1919-1921. I could write about frosts, about snow, another winter's effect on nature. About hemorrhoids and cold backs. About infected gums and frozen potatoes. About thin cereal and traces of blood on the snow. About chopping wood.

Uncle Lyosha says that everything here reminds him of Altay. He served a term in the '80s there. The same wood chopping, the profound silence, frostbitten fingers and legs that are cold to the bones.

We go together to fell trees. The old man skillfully cuts down the trees. We pull the logs to the truck. Then, near the bunkers, we saw, chop, and put it all in bags.

We are grateful for the wood that stands along our flanks, that our backup forces are cutting down a kilometer behind us. And I must admit that it is dangerous to go there.

First, we cut down the old dry trees, and then just any others. Mostly acacias. The trunks of the trees are riddled with splinters and bullets so that the chains on the saws break as if they are being used for heavy duty hauling. *Zzzz-snap! Zzzz-snap!*

"Come here," Uncle Lyosha gestures. His bright blue coat contrasts with the white field. He is easily spotted from a distance. He walks through the pristine snow, sweating and cursing. We follow behind him. We step firmly yet carefully. Who knows what gifts can be waiting for us to be in these woodlands.

"You yellow-toothed roosters," the old man says gloomily, but his face lights up instantly. He looks at me. "So, Artem, shall we smoke?"

I take out a blue Camel. He calls them fashionable cigarettes. *Zzzz-snap!*

This winter is unique in my life. If I don't stay in control, I can lose my sense of time and my sense of self and my life could become like that of field dust. Or acacia. Or ferns. Something without time, without sense, without emotion. You have to make up our own framework for your life to survive. Among your obligations, you do guard duty every day. You stand on duty, you sleep. Once every two weeks, you go to get more wood.

We return to the broken, frozen ground; the wind is cold, our feet are swollen, and our heads are clear. And then we stand near Uncle Lyosha's bunker, we wait, until water comes to a boil, we drink coffee and listen to stories. With these routines, life becomes controllable, and this means that you are in control, you're not falling apart, you're holding on. The most important thing is not to give in to laziness. The most important thing is to control and count the evenings. Not to sleep until noon. Not to eat after eight. Not to drink more than three shots. Not to forget to call your mother every Wednesday. Not to get too lazy to crawl out into the freezing cold and wind to scout the area with the infrared camera. To clean up the bunker before things get too messy. To brush your teeth at least once a day. To bathe at least once a week. To not smoke more than two packs a day. Then we'll make it. We stand around. We smoke. The old man remembers the 90s, the local gangsters, the North and Prima unfiltered cigarettes.

"Now the pigs rake everything in. Druggies for sure, I agree. It's true. Cocks and druggies."

"Tyomochka," Uncle Lyosha uses an affectionate form of my name, pulls at me with this gnarled fingers. "Give this old man a pack of fashionable cigarettes."

"And will the old man heat up the bath water?" I ask.

"These Kyivites. You're con men, not people!"

So I guess we came to an agreement.

This winter is long and threatening. It is wet and raw. It is quiet and dangerous. It's good to spend these kinds of winters at war. Or in a forest, for example, hidden from society. Or if worst comes to worst, in your summer home, among common people who are painfully forced to think of socialism. Or of the 90's. Or their barefoot childhood. For sure their barefoot childhood because it is only us, the fashionable ones, the Kyivites that spent our childhood in sandals. I go back to my area. In the bunker it smells of canned meat. Vlad and Sanya are heating up some pea soup with pork on the stove. There are also pickles, carp in liter jars, a bottle of Zubrowka, a box of mandarin oranges, and the seventh and eighth seasons of *Supernatural*.

Silence

I stop socializing. More than that, I stop talking. Oh, maybe accidentally I exchange some words: "Hi, what are you up to?", "Sure, oh, OK"… We hardly ever even speak to each other in our bunker. Everyone keeps to themselves. Some watch a movie, I write. Or also watch. And then write some more. And then go to my post… It seemed like that would be the place to talk, but we are silent, as if we are afraid of disturbing the cold quiet night. As if we aren't friends. As if we just met. Even though we know everything about one another. Even more than that. I'm silent, I have a process, the men don't distract me. They are tactful. They understand. Or maybe they just don't care. I sleep a lot at night and again I am silent. I just don't have the habit of talking in my sleep.

In the morning, I walk around the perimeter. I noticed that spring was coming. Even the scents were different. The air smelled of earth and wet trees. My eyes are getting used to not seeing white but really miss seeing green. Just like being on a long sea voyage. But instead of water there is soil. And the pirates are closer than the horizon.

Near Uncle Lyosha's bunker, I met Uncle Lyosha. We stood around, were quiet, smoked. He is one of us. Then Vusaty, the driver of the truck, walked up to us. He just winked, but said nothing. The three of us stood around.

I went back to my dugout, put on my headphones, and started a movie that I hadn't finished. But after some time I heard that something was falling not far away, most likely someone was firing an automatic grenade launcher.

"Let's go look," I suggested to my fellow soldiers.

"At what?"

"The war."

We climbed out of the dugout, stood at the edge of the outpost, right next to the field. Everyone around us was busy at work. And we just stood there, silent. Spitting.

Why should we walk? With whom? About what? We have already said everything. And we have already given up everything, the only thing left is silence.

Winter Crops

In October they told us that the commander of the company deserted. Moreover, obviously, this captain crossed to the side of the enemy. We had to be careful now, attentive and ready at any moment to encounter enemy scouts who, from now on, would know all our secret paths, the location of our posts, and even our birthdays.

For five months, we had lived with the information that the traitor commander was sitting one kilometer away and spying on us with new Russian binoculars, laughing into the collar of his new Russian overcoat, smoking stinky Russian cigarettes like Troika or Peter the Great. Truth be told, some of us didn't believe that the captain crossed to the side of the Russia-backed insurgents. This couldn't have happened. He was politically informed and had a moral compass. We wanted to think that he was in Poland, in some beat-up garage, repairing old Volkswagens. Either way, the captain disappeared, taking his weapons with him.

As soon as the snow melted, the orders came from above: Move forward. No, not with weapons, simply forward. With shovels. This is what we call occupying no man's land: when you create a system of trenches almost touching your enemy; when in your binoculars you can see the barcode on his canned meat and catch the timid glances of the two-headed eagle, the Russian national emblem, on the enemy's insignia; when you almost have an anxiety attack; when you get nervous not only from the large caliber shells but also from the continual fire from the other side; and every five minutes you check to see whether or not you removed your weapon's safety.

We moved forward. Almost along the whole front line. Some moved three hundred meters, some five, some a kilometer.

And then soldiers from the next regiment cleared the bush. Just as it should be: first the sappers deactivated mines, then the grunts went ahead and started digging. As soon as sappers entered a birch forest nearby, the radio transmitted the voice of Kurochka from the Bomb Disposal Unit:

"We got a body in the forest. Not fresh."

This happens to scouts and BDU guys a lot, discovering bodies in the bush. They might be some, not very cautious, locals who got caught up in the fire (doesn't matter from which side), or soldiers who never made it to their troop's location. It happened when our soldiers' bodies, supposedly those who disappeared back in the summer of 2014, were found. This time, it was that very same captain. His head shot by his own Makarov, his body half-eaten by foxes.

I'd been thinking about him for a few days. Because, you see, we even pronounced him a traitor, a deserter, a car mechanic; but as it turns out, he just shot himself through the head back in October, and was now resting here in the birch forest, food for Donbas animals. He lay like that for half the fall, the whole winter, now part of spring. He would have been still lying here were it not for our orders to move forward. Nobody had gone into the forest for a year and a half, and wouldn't now. There are enough IEDs there per square kilometer to decorate the Rockefeller Center Christmas tree. And he was lying there. While we here, in the dirt, in the thaw, in the frost, were sawing wood, digging ground, shooting at those who shot at us; while we went on vacation and treated our winter depression with Nutella; while we were thoughtlessly rotting in our bunkers and finishing the tenth season of Supernatural – he was lying there. Half-eaten by foxes.

But why foxes, specifically? Did someone stage a crime? Why not hares, or, perhaps, wild boars? Technically, it doesn't matter. Back in the summer, the rumor was that the captain was not right in the head. Kolya from the town of Ladyzhyn said he had a screw loose. Most considered him to be somewhat off, and our division medic was inclined to diagnose him as bipolar. He had no family. No desire to live either, it seems. So why not spend the winter in this extravagant way?

I felt no sympathy, and even less fear, but more responsibility. And the thought that crept in was a wily thought: I'm glad it's not me.

Lethargy

Back in June, when they brought us over to the rookies, "Katso," our sergeant who was scheduled to be demobilized in a few months, spoke about his patriotism, which the army destroyed. He spoke on a regular basis, conservatively and cynically.

I stood then, listened and didn't understand. "Either patriotism exists," I thought, "or it doesn't." You're a volunteer that came to defend your county, you couldn't do otherwise (there was no other way) and now you talk about patriotism. What patriotism when the enemy is "at the gate"? Today is exactly six months since we've been at the front. The enemy is still at the gate. But it was almost obvious to everyone that he is not only on the other side of the field.

And everyone seems to be fighting for the same idea, for the same goal, but in the end you still find yourself just a common soldier. And the head commander of this whole carnival is her majesty the Soviet Union. It's not about precise last names.

Here the whole system is greedy. Favoritism and uncontrolled, unbridled greed: beginning with a place for discharging weapons and ending with visits of officers to the sector of brigade commanders for whom in one neighboring position they even walked on the army equivalent of red carpets procured just for the purpose of greeting. And where were they when the soldiers swam in mud? And where were they when we melted ice so we could wash our balls at least once a week? And is it clear to them that your adequate soldier, on the front, never removed a cartridge from its magazine? You don't know who, when, and from what side they'll attack you.

And there are endless examples of this, and anger is often bordering on rebellion. And you only hear from the fighters: "Did all of you go crazy?"

And here I am – almost demobilized (even though I feel that I might have to serve a few extra months), lazy and tired, like Ziusudra who survived the flood. And I served those ten months honestly. Without wavering or getting drunk. With total commitment and a full bag on my shoulders. I helped all I could, through volunteers, acquaintances, friends: I didn't steal a single hryvnia, not one can of sardines packed in tomato sauce, not one drop of gasoline (with the exception of solar power to start the stoves); I didn't betray, mislead, run away, or stray off track. And it seems that everything should be getting better, that patriotism should be growing and flourishing, that hopes of happiness and testaments of the Kobzar growing and flourishing, that society should be becoming more discerning and informed that light should have victory over darkness. But I'm not blind and I don't think I'm stupid. I see everything, I understand everything. I feel everything. Most of all I feel waves of concrete covering up my patriotism, just like when in Woody Allen films it covers the bodies of dead gangsters put there by their killers. These waves flow, like boredom, they are heavy, they pull me to the bottom there where it all started. To the peaceful drinking of coffee beneath umbrellas, possibly before the Orange Revolution and before the student hunger strike of 1990, sometimes called the first Maidan.

It's likely that after demobilization I will forget the worst parts of this, what I will remember my service, and that I will regard this bureaucratic garbage with its blatant defects like the lesson the teacher chooses when she is being observed and the students must come in their pressed uniforms.

"Kids, who wants to talk about the hard lives of the greatest bards? And now everyone together: I am joining the ranks of all Soviet pioneer organizations named after Vladimir Illich Lenin in the presence of all my comrades, I solemnly swear."

And so, the concrete flows over me, breaking my bones and causing internal bleeding. Again and again. And here it is – the ninth time head down. Into the whirlpool. To the bottom. Feet in the sludge. Like a year in a cryogenic chamber in lethargic sleep. To forget or just not to know.

Inescapable Experience

Strange things happen to us. Sometimes just unexpected or strange or unexpected and strange at the same time. Then we say: it was a learning experience. Everything becomes a valuable experience. I had such an amazing experience. I was mugged by gypsies on the train – an experience. A customer failed to pay me – an experience. I embarrassed myself at someone's house – an experience. We calm ourselves with this handy word that can be applied to every situation, we justify most of our humiliations and failures with it, as if that's what was needed for us to grow and learn – an experience.

Sometimes I feel bad that something didn't happen to me. The kinds of things that can happen only once in your lifetime. It can't happen again. The stars won't align themselves in that constellation again.

I envied Sanya B.'s experiences at some level.

It was a cool but tender morning in the beginning of April. It seemed that only Valera, the chaplain, and I knew that it was Sanya's birthday.

It was only our second turn. We would change guard duties at night. We were to serve at the distant watch point. There were six of us. Including Sanya B., but he was missing from the group of us that was going out to take our daily turn on duty. Near Sanya's dugout, beneath the body of a broken tank, in which, according to the legend you could still hear the voices of the crew that died (I even learned their names later), stood a pale Klim mumbling something super quickly, flailing his arms. We walked up and saw the horror on Klim's face and I became afraid myself. My first thought was: Sanya B. hanged himself.

But no, he didn't hang himself. And it wasn't Sanya B. On the steps that led down into the dark dugout, lay Stepan's one hundred kilogram body.

"Dead?" I asked.

"Cold," answered one of our boys.

Some of our group proceeded to the guard post while some stayed to wait for the official investigators.

At the guard post near the fire was a busy, calm, and as always intent, Sanya B.

"Happy birthday," I said. "Was it you who killed Stepan?"

"I don't need that," Sanya B. answered. "It was just that the first thing I saw this morning, on my birthday, was a corpse. It made me want to run away."

"And you ran here."

"Yes," he said.

"That's some experience," I replied automatically.

"This is bullshit," Sanya B. said. "I'm going to go into the city tomorrow to buy a cake. I don't want alcohol. We don't need it."

"We don't need it," I repeated.

I fell deep into thought. About the corpse on the steps of the dugout on a birthday. About cheap Popasna cakes that give you heartburn. About our distant outpost, where you are closer to the snipers than to your own people. How quickly will you die? Are you ready to die? And was Stepan ready to die? Last time I saw him was in camp. He came out of the bushes, swollen from alcohol, red, dirty, covered with sores and scabs, with his pants down and underwear wet in the groin.

I sat against the bulwark (will a caliber 12 or 7 go through that stump?) and I thought about death. Well, and about the experience, which, strangely enough, Sanya B. had. Not for me, but for him. I celebrated my thirtieth birthday on the bus on the way to the Crimean border. I had a fever of forty centigrade and every two hours I swallowed a horse's dose of Acetaminophen. Sanya B. was luckier. On this thirty-first birthday, he saw a corpse. What does that mean? Maybe it means good luck. Or maybe it means a long life… And in twenty years he'll tell his kids about it… But no, he won't. It's me who would've talked about it. Because for me this would be an experience, but for him it's bullshit.

And also, I thought, maybe my own death would be – a questionable experience. But, eventually, inescapable. Then it all seemed to me to be very wise and appropriate.

A Lifetime and a Little More

"Have you been here for a long time, guys?" we asked.

Six months.

Wow.

God, how long ago that was. We stood by empty dugouts, looking at the field of sunflowers up ahead, with ravines and forests illuminated by the pre-dawn sun behind us. These belonged to us. And beyond the field – that was not ours, at least not yet. Don't ever go there, it's full of mines and booby traps, the guys from the 54th brigade told us, they jumped into a cargo van and got the hell out of there, leaving us alone in the field with boxes of ammunition and a super long winter.

"Six months," we thought. "That's almost an entire lifetime. Six months on the front, a whole spring and summer under fire, without even minimal daily living conditions, stuck in the gray earth. Well, those boys are heroes. Really – heroes!"

And so autumn went by and after it – winter. Our bunkers leaked like bleeding icons, we swam in mud, we struggled with sunken technical equipment – froze on observation posts, killed lice on the food from headquarters and in our mattresses. How long have we been here? Already seven months.

Are we heroes? Of course not. We can stand to be here just as long again. And we can go past the field, over the field, and further if necessary. Seven months. This is longer than a lifetime. This is a lifetime, and a little more. Because here it is – spring, with new life, new hopes, experiences, where there is room for despair, and sadness, and also some kind of lighthearted joy from the greening of the shrubs and trees. And finally, it's such a high to go to the outhouse in slippers instead of rubber boots.

Seven months on the front – that's when you understand everything, but you have no desire to speak, when speaking isn't necessary, but you understand everything. When you know what your fellow soldiers are thinking by their facial expressions. When quiet alerts you and gun fire and explosions rearrange everything. When a machine gun becomes not just a shooting instrument but your passport and your diploma testifying to your passing of all required higher education courses. When you miss your family so much that you just don't think about them so that you will not remind yourself again about that life, which you don't know how you lived until mobilization. We joke: rotation is for the weak. But most people want to go home. Just so that they can rest, catch up on sleep, so that they don't forget that they are not just a soldier, but also a human being, who can wash the dust and dirt of many long months off your skin. And then they can come back. Many plan to re-enlist, for many war has become a part of their lives, for some – the reason to be alive.

After serving – life is meaningless, depression, the inability to connect thoughts, and discomfort, as if you are wearing someone else's retainer or sleeping with crumbs in your bed.

"Hey guys," someone asks us. "Have you been here for a long time?"

"Seven (eight, nine) months."

"Wow."

"That's just normal," we say.

And we ourselves think, "It's really *wow*..."

We have been here a long time. All our lives, and more.

Cotard's Syndrome

Kostya believes in God and drinks a lot. Sometimes we don't see him for weeks. He doesn't climb out of the dugout, doesn't go to put on his uniform, doesn't go on guard duty, and doesn't interact with us. He doesn't even really have a proper dugout. It's more like a foxhole, where he obviously eats, drinks, and goes to the bathroom. In the event of a direct hit by an "80s generation" grenade on that hole he along with all his prayers would be turned into minced meat. But he's not worried about that, he just continues to live, or more accurately to exist, drinking away the taxpayers' money. Three times a month he goes into the city with a huge industrial sack, fills it with bottles of alcohol and returns to his position. He crawls into the dugout and drinks. What he eats is uncertain. Probably, pastries from a box. Once I saw him carrying a sixty-liter bottle of sunflower oil into the dugout. Kostya is like an animal. Dirty and unshaven, hair full of burrs, untrimmed nails, dirty weapons, a mad look, and a frightening smile. In the course of a half a year on the front, he has changed into a kind of dog, the kind that wanders into army camps with the hope of finding some leftovers to eat.

And so, coming back from duty at the front line, we see a deranged Kostya run up and down our encampment, anxiously babbling under his breath that his heart isn't beating. More precisely, that it has totally disappeared. "It killed me," Kostya explains in a panic. *A mine killed me and now I don't have a heart.* He ran up to Uncle Lyosha to ask for advice, looked into the dugouts, grabbed his chest, took off his sweater to show off his shaven body with the long scar from his stomach to his solar plexus, shook out his hair as if removing sand, and dramatically sat down on the ground, wailing like a small child, after which he quickly got up and ran again.

We call the platoon's paramedic. A good guy and a cynic, the 23-year-old "doc" calmly goes up to Kostya, stops him, takes him by the hand, takes his pulse, looks him in eyes, and sets him on the ground.

"Idiot," the doc says with suppressed alarm in his voice. "You have problems. You don't have a heart." Then he comes up to us. He says that Kostya most likely is experiencing delirium tremens. He assures us that tomorrow they'll take him away.

"But it might be better to shoot him," he adds. "I'm joking. Though not really."

Kostya returns to his dugout and seems to fall asleep. Well, we didn't hear him for a couple of hours. And then we heard him. He cried loudly, so frighteningly, like a man cries, in pain, with reverberating and increasing force. He cried for a long time. Until night, it seemed. Then, they say, he ran again, cut the skin on his chest, showed off some old mortar fragments, as if they killed him. I check the Internet. Enter the symptoms. All that Google can come up with in response to my search is Cotard's Syndrome. The first symptom is the patient's certainty that they are missing some organs. "People with Cotard's syndrome," I read, "may think that their brain is decaying, that they lost some internal organs, or that they melted. Some are even certain of the fact that they are walking around dead."

The next day they took Kostya to the "madhouse." They injected him, treated him for something. It seems like kidney failure, which, as they write about in the medical literature, can provoke the same syndrome.

And then they discharged him as an "avatar," which means as an alcoholic, without finishing his treatment. "It would have been better if they had shot him," I thought then. What became of him? I'm afraid to even imagine. He probably died. From the lack of a heart.

A Quasi-Religious Worldview

"Artem, what are you doing, bitch?"

"What's it to you?"

Uncle Lyosha, dressed in white summer army underwear, a wool blanket around his waist, and rubber boots, stands across from us. His eyes are bloodshot, his hands appear to be itching for a fight, and he is smiling, but there is a hint of danger about him.

"Artem," he says. "How about tomorrow you chop wood."

"And today?"

"Today is Sunday. On Sundays work is forbidden." He regards me not only as a close neighbor but also as a grandson – it is the only thing that saves me from his constant ridicule and his habitual manipulation. I sense this. Sometimes I even use it to my advantage...

Prison rules, like in religion, become the religion of the prisoners. Let's say, what can a person achieve in sixty years of life, what understanding, what meaning, and what great truths can they use to fill their inner world? Uncle Lyosha, who is a tough man, has his own perceived understandings of justice. They have been warped by the harshness of camp experiences. And his understanding is tightly interwoven with the rules of prison life and religious rituals. This is when you can take an eye out for, let's say, spitting inside the house or cut an ear off for homosexuality. "You work on Sunday, it's the noose for you. I'll break your leg over this, bitch. Which hand do you use to cross yourself, you scum? Forcefully enforced!"

This world – it's as if it's speaking to you, an abstract metaphoric experience of strangers. This world, filled with Flemish proverbs that frighten with their incomprehensibility and mysteriousness. You are not very knowledgeable about these laws – prison, religion, laws of justice, and scholastic morals.

In my discussions with Uncle Lyosha, I usually agree with everything he says. I usually don't argue with him, honoring his need to be right. Arguing for my version of truth is not something I feel I need to do.

"You know what, old man," I say to him, "for some reason I was certain that today was Saturday."

"A Jewish day of rest. But we are not Jewish."

I agree. Well, I don't really agree, but I don't argue. More accurately, I don't agree with the rhetoric, which totally ignores the essence of what was said. His understanding – is based on religion, and religion dictates his understanding. I wonder if he remembers what is actually written in the Bible and what was only transmitted orally from generation to generation in his world of incarceration.

But I accept some part of his belief system It's strange. For example, to spit inside a house is disgusting. And as for name calling, you always have to be held accountable. It isn't hard; more than that, it gives structure to your life, gives you simple and clear answers to difficult questions, provides meaning to meaningless events, gives you a reason to exist, makes clear the difference between good and evil, defines order and chaos, and raises anthropocentrism to be the guiding principle of life on earth. Don't work on Sunday, don't steal from your friends, don't get too high, honor thy mother and thy father. And, of course, remember, what is acceptable and what is not. The list is not very long. The most important thing is to be consistent. And to be honest with yourself. So religion, just like the prison system of rules, demands honesty and routine.

Such People, Such Rocks

If the war has become insignificant to those who live south of the wall, it is even worse than for those who have lived through it for many months. I don't want to write about it, I want to forget.

This is like life in the Soviet Union.

And then there are those crazies who are called and attracted to focus on the damaged areas and towns close to the front with toppled statues of Lenin and broken windows and hospitals hit by artillery fire by our own battalions. It's as if some Western journalist or some community activist read his fill of leftists like the French writers Henri Barbusse, Andre Gide, or the German-Jewish writer Lion Feuchtwanger about the Soviet Union. "Let me live there. This country, these people are strong!" And he comes and he is surprised by everything and he finds some things oppressive, and he finds some things shocking. And the people, such people... gulag, ballet, traditions, some kind of work meetings, demonstrations... And, captivated, he writes about everything, gives interviews to his western colleagues, and then a year passes, then two, and life in the Soviet Union becomes an unpleasant routine, a stagnant pool, with no entry into the sea, a moldy rivulet, in which an unsteady flag holds the existence of the entire platoon.

"Well, what it is like there?" they ask him. "This is the Soviet Union, this country, these people are strong."

"Well, you're wrong. People are people. The country is like any other country. The gulag, the state apparatus, crooks, deficit. This isn't interesting."

"At all?"

"At all."

And this is the way I feel about some of the volunteers or just random visitors.

"We went to the war zone! And they are shooting there, and people are rocks over there."

Well, yes, they shoot, well these people are more honest (compelled to be) than ordinary citizens.

Parched skin, clothing soiled to bare recognition, fatigue and determination reflected in murky eyes. And nothing amazes them anymore and nothing shocks anymore. Who is interested in all of this? What should I write about it?

Our Anniversary
Somewhere in the Donbas

How long has it been since I've seen her? It used to be that even a week away from her seemed like an eternity. Even when we were tired of each other, tired of our cramped living quarters, when it seemed that she was me and so all possible secrets were revealed in their entirety. Even then I started to quickly miss her. We had been together ten years, and in the coming days it would be our anniversary and it has been the longest time that I have been away from her: three months.

Her new book came out and the publisher organized a book tour of Ukraine. I didn't publish anything for five years and this doesn't bother me one bit, but her book is partly mine too. There was a lot of me in there, a lot of our shared experiences, and of course, a shared pain permeates her poems. And so the next place on the list of her tour is Northern Donetsk. It's about fifty kilometers away from here, almost right next to us, one region dissected with checkpoints along the road.

I want to go, but I also don't want to, I'm afraid. Mainly, I'm afraid to disrupt the comfortable daily routine that I have created for myself, the predictable pattern, the hourly schedule of my life, the understanding of events. The kind of trip that would cause me such inner turmoil, like an unexpected whirlwind that knocks all boats off their prescribed course. But Vlad convinces me, explains the necessity of this journey, explains as best he can – simply and without sentiment. And I hardly understand any of his words, but he insists.

Petrovych, from the same platoon as me, calmly lets me go. The taxi driver agrees to drive me for four hundred hryvnias. Uncle Lyosha says that I shouldn't come back until it's been at least a week, he says that there isn't anything that needs to be done, that the separatists won't disappear while I'm gone and I should rest, catch up on sleep, and spend time with my wife of course.

On the road from our position (Zolote, Hirske, Bila Hora, Lycychansk) and all the way to Northern Donetsk, I was as nervous, as if before a first date. The taxi driver went on about our predecessors, about the boys from the 54th, how he helped them and even went with them to fight, but unfortunately the relationship with them didn't work out (even though they were regular boys, drank in moderation, and not crazy?). He explained about the boys that they killed under the town of Troitsky. He made comments about mines and the combines that we passed, he talked about the separatist fighters he knew, who got tired of fighting a long time ago and want to spend their retirement peacefully in the Soviet Union. While passing Hirske, he pointed out three girls near the road close to the pharmacy.

Why do you have to go so far? We have everything here and it's cheaper than in Northern Donetsk.

I explained to him that I was going to see my wife. He apologized, and asked whether I wanted to stop at the bakery to buy a cake.

The end of April is my favorite time of year. It's when something new always stirs inside me. It's when every year I feel some kind of magical connection with the earth, something that takes my breath away and makes me glad to be alive – a force that is the opposite of evil. The white blossoming of pears, the green grass on the hills, the fresh *chornozem* on private lawns, the wonderful sun and the fear of the unknown and forgotten create a kind of amazing picture, that stirs up many emotions in me that were lost throughout this year, spent in an atmosphere of nullification.

I go to her, as if for the first time, to the unfamiliar, unknown. Like ten years ago when I asked her to go to Lviv for the weekend, even though she had never seen me beyond the limits of our virtual conversations. Then I also went to the railroad station in a *marshrutka*, with a similar feeling of silent fear and thirsty interest.

At 4 p.m., I stand near that same restaurant. She runs outside, embraces me, says something, pulls me inside, "Let's go, I'll introduce you." People sit there, finishing their meals. A collection of local patriots, her publisher, and one other poet who can't see well, and it seems he can hardly understand what he is doing there and who all these people are.

I order soup, *kotlety*. I sit and chew and don't know how to get used to the surroundings. Some kind of thick fog, strange scents, people, chairs, dishes on the menu, music, and I am in the mountains with sewn patches of Saint Michael and the flag of Ukraine. I haven't shaved in two days, I have dirt on my hands that doesn't immediately wash away, and am uncomfortably sweaty. I am lost in the end.

Two days. We have two days. She seems happy, but as for me, even though I try to feel the same way, I lapse into a numb stupor all the time.

Nothing makes me happy, I don't desire anything. It would be better to go back, to a daily predictable life, to the narrow stairs of the dugouts, to the damp scent, to the anticipation of slight danger on duty every day, to the schedule, to the planning out, to the togetherness, to the mutual understanding. To the deep desire not to be there, but to be with her.

We eat breakfast somewhere, go to the movies, walk around the city, drink limoncello in the apartment that we rented for two days, where someone left new orthopedic inserts for army boots on the radiators. She laughs or suddenly bitterly cries in the middle of the street – she lost her earring. Later she finds it in the wrinkled sheets.

I sleep a lot. Even during the day I managed to fall asleep for several hours. I try to be good, the one who she waited to see. But for me this, stubbornly, doesn't work.

Through the window the leaves rustle in a cozy way. During the day when I am leaving the rain doesn't stop falling – that same kind of spring rain, that brings with the water happiness and light sadness.

It's good that I was able to get away, I say at the bus station. She is going to Slovyansk and I am going to Popasna. It's good that we had this. You and I are on our anniversary somewhere in Donbas.

This will be something to remember and something to tell our children.

"Lord," I think, "There will be so much to tell our children that there won't be enough time in our lives to tell it all."

Seventeen Bags of *Paskas*

At the beginning of May volunteers from Vinnytsya come again. We asked them not to bring anything except mineral water, but that "except mineral water" meant a cart full of stuff that a simple soldier, to tell the truth, could easily live without. Several boxes of candy, fruit, batteries, some pies and cheesecakes, herring in buckets and canned sardines, a large supermarket bag full of underwear and seventeen bags of *paskas*, an Easter bread.

It was a few days after Easter. The boys were let go from fourth rotation, some made their way into the infirmary, and some went on leave. At the outpost together with the regular servicemen about thirty people were left. It had already been a month since we captured a kilometer for the gray zone and built new fortifications there. A portion of our personnel were permanently stationed on the borders, so that there was hardly anyone at the outpost. Come and take it with your bare hands, cut down the sleeping and drunk soldiers in their bunkers. But that's not the point. Despite the number of soldiers at headquarters here, they brought us about twenty *paskas*. More than enough. We wouldn't need more. What's more, Uncle Lyosha's volunteers sent some full boxes also. *Paskas*, eggs, sausage, cheese, ham. Someone also received a package from home. Someone else made a special trip to Popasna and bought some. It was as if all of Ukraine waited for Easter, so that they could fill the front line with food. Enough to make us sick. Enough to support the country. Enough to suffocate us.

And also there came some people from Vinnytsya again with a van crammed full of stuff.

Guys, go back, guys! Leave us one bag and take the rest back. We can't eat it all, sorry, we said.

What do you mean you can't eat it all? The guys were amazed. You have seventy healthy mouths here. Eat, boys, eat.

What seventy? There were seventy in the winter, and now there aren't even thirty.

Eat, they said firmly.

And then they left. So calm, so sure of themselves and satisfied that they fulfilled their mission to feed the soldiers.

We put the *paskas* under a canopy by the generator. Seventeen garbage bags. Twenty pieces in each one. Still fresh. A little crushed, but fresh. It reminded us of the time we had to throw bacon into the stoves and we had to throw whole moldy wheels of cheese into trenches, but we will try to eat them (yes, yes, there were times, when there was so much cheese and bacon, that we had to throw it out.) It used to be that they gave each soldier three kilograms of hard cheese a week. And on top of that hundreds of cans of conserved beef and condensed milk with which we built whole pyramids. And aside from that time, at other times it wasn't that necessary. But we couldn't stomach more than one *paska* in a day for three of us. The rest, having their own stashes, totally refused to take them.

We were eating. Slowly. After a week we saw that all we managed to do was to finish three bags. And the rest? Some started to go bad, to dry out, to get moldy. One bag got caught in the rain, and we had to get rid of that gooey mess. And we had to go to the gray zone, because the war would get louder by the day. Several days in a row we ate only *paska*, we randomly added chocolate candy to our rations, and at some point we realized that our urine already smells of vanilla. We had to go back to kasha. With great satisfaction we ate a couple of cans of stew.

But some *paskas* were still left. And that turned into a big problem since most of us had grown up with the idea that we shouldn't even waste a crumb on the floor. We could casually throw away a bucket or two of kasha, or hide a few bags of potatoes in the *chornozem*. But not bread. Not even a crust should be thrown out, or the earth herself would curse us, and the grain farmers would pursue us, with their calloused hands, to our very end. Ukraine lived through the Holodomor, an artificial famine, in 1930s, and nobody forgot about it. Wasting bread was blasphemy, a sacrilegious act. We looked at the bags sadly. The bread, made from the rich Ukrainian earth, was rotting. We looked at the way the bags stood there looking so pathetic, eaten away by mice here and there, how the disturbed spirits of the native farmers hovered above them and their salty sweat and fatigue of living go to the dogs. My friend Roman found a solution; for a long time he had been going to the village located at the front line. He would obtain milk, cheese, sour cream and vodka from the villagers there. He carried the *paskas* on his shoulders himself. Let the cows and chickens eat them. He made several trips there, and one day he was surprised by an ambush. Startled, he discharged his magazine and carefully made it back still carrying the bread...

And then we telephoned the people from Vinnytsya.

"Well, so, did you eat everything?"

"We ate everything," we lie.

"So, you know what, next week we'll come again!"

"No," we replied coarsely.

I hope that they weren't offended.

Watching Out for the Enemy

Somehow from the beginning I was watching out for the enemy. That is, at this position. Life in an open space dictates its own rules. Sometimes you can avoid following them, you can defy fate, live in spite of it, against all odds. But you can't avoid watching out for the enemy. In a month this becomes an automatic reflex. Always looking out at the field, surveying the clumps of green thickets. There, where they're shooting from. Where they are coming from. Sometimes I noticed that except for the guards no one ever watches out for the enemy the whole day long. Sometimes even the guards don't look. They don't care about life. After all, death is something that happens to other people.

Entering the military, I made myself a clear goal: to survive. And if necessary – to die. But to remain alive. That necessity still hasn't happened, so my goal is to always watch out for the enemy. Every day, while waking, I go take a leak in the bushes. Then I watch for the enemy. Sitting on a pallet with a cut-out hole and swatting away flies – I look around. Sunbathing, I scan the area between the field and my post.

I train almost daily. Dumbbells, weights, oak logs, pull up bars, strengthening exercises. My focus is on schooling myself. The subject is the enemy. I train and watch. It suddenly occurs to me: Is there someone on the enemy's side who also is training and watching our positions? He lifts weights, eats energy bars, goes out for morning runs. Or maybe he just sits, extremely bored, watches for fires on our side and thinks: What do those Ukrainians do? What do they live on? Are all of them drunk or only half? Maybe they're eating? And what do they eat? Those children of Donbas? Maybe they are sleeping in their bunkers watching movies? Which movies?

Which ones? Of course, we watch one and the same thing. Just a kilometer away we sit under a sign or behind a wall and watch the latest news. Pirated, with bad sound, with Joy Casino commercials. Action flicks – usually action flicks – usually about the current heroes, and we laugh at these films because we know how to hold the weapons and how to use them, and the actors and directors obviously don't. We know that even the smallest wound raises the temperature of your body to forty degrees, that the pitch of a shot from a Kalashnikov – is nothing, that the RPG-7 is capable of stopping any kind of technology, and that after three hits on an armored vehicle the idiot usually won't crawl out of it happy and smiling.

They released red flares. They are always releasing them, but after that almost always nothing ever happens. It happens spontaneously, without warning. And I look. Keep watch. I know the real story about the outposts that were cut down. I know the stories about dugouts full of mines. I know that at night the scouts move like boar. They move all the same. That's why I keep watch.

Everyday when I go to the water station to fill up the twenty-liter plastic bottle with water, I turn my head to the left – I look at the enemy. When I return with the bottle to the bunker – I turn my head to the right. Every night sitting by the fire, I squint, try to peer through the evening fog into the field, to the place I am studying on the other side. Before sleep, I slip outside to breathe, into the night. Always, being out in an open space and watching – over there. Life without a proper roof over our heads dictates its rules. It's impossible not to keep them.

A Unique Spring

This spring is unique in my life. It's probably worth writing a separate story about it. Something in the spirit of Pirandello and Beckett at the same time. About the drama of everyday life, about its philosophical foundation, about the unavoidable failures in life, about escape from reality. The spring began with silence. Quiet March days filled with a kind of muted quiet and the lack of desire to talk. Black crows and ravens circling above, last year's grass dry but damp, the mucky *chornozem*, scorching sun, frost, and an endless number of films that I watched over and over again, from morning until late into the night. And also those same preparations for capturing the gray zone, the unmotivated escape of a combatant after the explosion of a grenade and the wounding of Sanya, the first night of initiation, where I secretly wrote my will.

And also deaths, other wounding, Yura's black coat, our banner, three packs of cigarettes a day and a Black energy drink by the liter.

This spring of endless training, five times a week. Of trying to eat healthy. Cereal, milk, bananas, eggs, fish, everything we buy for ourselves in Popasna.

I write a lot. I only part with my tablet during training sessions. Writing and training are both activities that prevent me from going crazy, things that keep my head above water, that help me understand my needs. Above all for myself.

This spring left me with an emotional emptiness and a brotherly love for my fellow mates. Everything on daily duty becomes routine. There is you, the weapons, a shabby mattress pulled from an abandoned house, there is a radio, "observation tower," "bush," "binoculars," "infrared camera," nightingales, and quiet. You go about two meters to take a leak and you have the impression that your pissing was heard in Luhansk.

Listen, keep listening, look into the night, look at the silent field. Or at the dark and cold sky. "Do you see a drone? It sees you."

It sometimes seems that everyone can see you from the other side. And most likely has you in their PSO telescopic sniper sight. Even when you are looking through a PSO at the same time. Even when you sleep on the shabby mattress, someone sees you. They can sneak around from behind. Between you are:

1. An army field telephone TA-57.

2. An optical sniper's sight.

Only a kilometer of bush separates you from them. A distance from which you can be shot. You and the four other soldiers on duty with you. And in case of an attack you won't even have time to reposition your DShK 1 machine gun. Won't have time to grab your PKM machine gun. So you must always keep your own weapons ready. And your heart *thumps-thumps-thumps* from nicotine, caffeine, and of course, adrenaline. And your feet are frozen in boots or sneakers. And then the long awaited dawn arrives, when the demons and monsters disappear with the first rays of the sun that save you from nightmares. Then a lot of strong coffee, Chinese food (sardines in tomato sauce with instant noodles), *paska* or candy, the hunting of rabbits, boar, and pheasants, and a long and fortunate path to the outpost, where there is sleep, a shower, training, books, films, and of course, writing.

This spring is like transparent air that fills the lungs. Quiet, disturbing, and yet even tender sometimes. It fills you with happiness because you managed to live through it, you didn't freeze in the snow piles and didn't get attacked by Donbas animals because those who were wounded got better and those who died were buried with honors. It hastened summer, it hastened the possibility of the coming demobilization, which it seems will never come, it gave us a tan and kvass to drink by the mine field, the cleanliness of a trained body and the smell of a submachine gun. It smells like wormwood in the bunker. Everybody in our small collective makes peace with one another and we spent the quiet mornings in Popasna cafés. This spring means sadness and unexpected meetings with dear people in the center of the oblast, and the chocolate-flavored protein leaves residue on my fingers.

This spring is unique. One that I have never experienced before and that I believe I will never experience again.

Prostitutes Are Always
Following the Army

Prostitutes are seldom appreciated for their skills and know-how. They are like assorted moths, attracted to distant faint army bonfires. And they are always nearby. Whether you like it or not.

Prostitutes are ready to engage in a dialogue, as if they are parliamentarians. They are ready to talk to you and tell you strange stories about their lives full of struggle and run-ins with cops. They are conscientious and loyal. They are honest and hungry. The prostitutes of Donbas are always hungry, and they eat at any opportunity. They eat canned food, pastries, they eat white bread with condensed milk, and frozen sweet potatoes. They like smoked chicken wings and pig ears, sausages with cheese, and sausages with bacon. They really love bacon. Ground bacon with garlic, a classic army spread that is packed into plastic containers and doled out, one kilogram per person, every week at the army field kitchen. They also love pea soup.

They wash the food down with vodka or beer, they get drunk easily, but they don't get full. And that is why they keep on eating. Prostitutes are sensitive. They can help a soldier struggling with depression, they understand the pain of loss and are prepared to pray for you at any moment. They pray as loudly as they sing. I have heard them praying and singing.

At six in the morning, only the guards are awake. On duty at distant outposts, the guards protect us as we sleep. How many of us are left? Twenty out of ninety. And I sleep, covered up in my sleeping bag with my head wrapped in a T-shirt so that bedbugs won't bite. I am awakened by a strange hoarse singing coming from outside. For one moment it seems to me that I have died, and that I am in purgatory: in this same bunker, but instead of the snoring of my friend I hear the hoarse singing of a woman. I climb out of the hole and wander to the washing area where I suddenly see her sitting on top of our tank in ripped jeans and a worn-out army T-shirt. She sits there singing.

Hello, I say. *Can't sleep, huh?*

She smiles revealing black teeth eaten away by cavities and doesn't answer. She goes on singing some Russian song about green waves, sailing ships and a storm after a hot day.

Who are you waiting for? I ask, shaking the cold drops of water from my hands, standing in the emerald patch of bushes lit by the morning rays of the sun.

Again, she doesn't answer.

It's clear who she is waiting for. Anyone who is desperate, or going crazy, the mowers of the Luhansk steppe that will return after their mission, tired and sweaty. At midnight they dug up the field with their tanks, their hands full of the scent of fish and nicotine, their dry lips cracked from thirst and drunkenness. But they will return, and she will be waiting for them, she who loves them more than her two kids, she who understands their pain and treats their depression and emotional instability.

She is just lonely, so she sits and waits. She is sad, so she sings despite the gunfire. She is used to explosions, she spends most of her time on the front line, in the damp dugouts, with those who provide her with alcohol and gifts from cooks, pharmacists, and from local city groceries. Prostitutes always follow the army, like dogs and cats. So where there are soldiers, along with pain and death, you will also find warmth and nourishment, and, of course, love.

Ode to New Balance

In my first hours in the army some careless sergeant issued me size 44 black boots. I wear size 43 and these were really gigantic. It seemed that an aluminum army flask could fit into the space between my toes and the toes of the boots. On my pointing out to the sergeant that the boots were too big, he just said: *Shove some grass in there.*

Aha, I thought, grass. And after a couple of hours I exchanged them for sneakers. Dark-green New Balance 891s. Then they were supposed to ship me summer boots that were three times as light as my issued ball and chain boot and ten times as comfortable. So until now I run in New Balance. Faster than anyone and better than anyone.

Of course, we only had to wear boots during formation so I usually wore my sneakers. And then when I finished initial training, and I was first sent to Haysyn to the hundredth division, and then to Henichesk, to my platoon. There we also had to wear boots for formation. And on guard duty. The rest of the time I wore the New Balance 891s. And then on the coast of the Sea of Azov, no one made you do anything at all because of a crazy heat wave. A heavy, humid kind of sea heat. I had some Crocs, which totally amazed everyone. I usually wore them, only at night I put on sneakers, careful not to step on a snake.

And then there was the training camp, Shyrokyi Lan. For 45 days I hardly took off the New Balance 891s: training, studying, running over parched steppes, dust and heat, sand and baked armor.

And then it was September. And now, bonded together and prepared, we set off to the east. I didn't take off the New Balance 891s until the frosts started, so not until the end of November, endlessly celebrating the way they lasted, their endurance, their quality, and love for me. They really loved me, as only a good and quality object can love its owner. Their laces didn't untie, they didn't rub my feet, they kept their shape and looked the same as they had a year and a half ago, when I bought them in the shopping center in Shuliavka.

In winter, I wore cheap boots, for one hundred and eighty hryvnias. They were not good for quick movement, but were warm, and were comfortable when worn on guard duty at night. Even at minus 25 the toes began to freeze only after three hours on duty.

And when the frosts ended and the snow melted I put on my sneakers again.

And I wore them in spring.

And in summer.

And in training.

And running.

And in drills.

And in assignments.

And in escaping.

And standing.

And falling.

And crawling.

And sleeping.

I dreamed of wearing them again when I returned. At home. On excavations or mushrooms hunts. Or just walking around the forest. Or even the city.

And now I have only a few weeks left to serve. Two? Three? And I am still wearing them. And they suit me, and they protect me. They served me well throughout the war. At the training camp, at the Sea of Azov, and will continue to serve me. They're good luck. I won't give them away, and more importantly, I won't throw them out until the soles wear out and the leather tears to pieces. You need to value such things. You must protect them the way they protected you. The way they saved you. And when the time comes that you get too lazy to clean them, remember, the way your fellow soldiers approached you and said: "Man, I envy you. You have such fucking amazing shoes."

The Abuse

I can understand those who say that this is not their war, that they didn't send me (us) over there, and overall, that this is a war of oligarchs – principled and unprincipled. I can understand those who say, "How is it going for you? I also say, 'I am also a patriot but I have rheumatism.'" I can understand those who say, "So I have a brother near Kramatorsk, who says, 'Things have quieted down and the war is probably ending.'" But I will never forgive those stationed at the checkpoints who think they are better than everyone else, almost forcing front line soldiers to kneel before them. They search vehicles and carry sniper rifles with silencers, with a lazy waddling gait and squinting eyes behind glasses.

"Who is this?"

And so, impoverished and alcohol-infused, the infantry troop drives home. One that was stuck in a swamp for five to ten months, that woke up to a *ba-bang* and fell asleep to the *tra-ta-ta,* one that washed once every two weeks, smeared with a caustic cream and cheap gasoline, drank tonics for various ailments, who after forty (or some after fifty) hours crawled on their bellies to relieve those at the guard post living on dry rations and stimulants, drinking Black energy drinks instead of water. So that it was possible not to sleep for forty hours. And here, thirty kilometers from the line, at the outpost a pig with a manicure jumps out and proceeds to be verbally abusive: your uniform doesn't meet regulations, or you are transporting too many things, or the stamp on your military ticket has rubbed off. "Why are you being so cocky, open your bags, take your shoes off. OK, you may go."

The infantry troop drives on, swallowing the disrespect, quickly forgetting about all the unpleasant incidents at the checkpoints. At home their wives are waiting for them. The day before the reunion they will go to their hair dressers, dye their hair copper, the color of rust, which their husbands so carefully remove from their weapons with rust remover. At home their kids are waiting for them, kids who won't be able to fall asleep the day before with worry and excitement. Their mothers are waiting for them, never sleeping because of anxiety and sadness.

And they also wait for those serving at the checkpoints. Those same kinds of wives, those same kinds of children, exhausted parents, happy colleagues. And in their pockets, those very same kinds of papers certifying their status as participants in military actions. Participants! So you took part. In the military actions. So you shot, you hid from death. In other words, you cheated death and returned home a hero. How many are there like you? We are so overjoyed by this. So happy. Thank you, Universe, for not having me serve at checkpoints surrounded by modified sniper rifles. Thank you for not dragging me off the train and sending me into the National Guard.

The End of the Fifth Tour

What has changed since then? Maturity, anger, fatigue? Maybe disillusionment? Experience? A new burden that we will have to live with? Foot fungus? Death? And then at the end of May, everything changed. They brought us all together from training at: Shyrokyi Lan, Rivne, Yavoriv, Cherkasy. They mixed us, shuffled us, turned us inside out (gave us our military ID tags with our military profession?) and scattered us throughout the southern steppes. Here we are. There is Crimea. Don't get the two mixed up. Crimea? The Black Sea? Did they mobilize us for this? To catch snakes, lizards, and drink local wines sold from the hoods of Lanos and Slavuta cars. Time dragged on, every day was completely packed full, so that it seemed that by summer's end we would also be done with our tour. Our eyes shone, like the hot glassy Sea of Azov, our skin turned as dry and yellow as the grass of Askania. And the guys there, near Maryinka! And those in the 72nd there near Volnovakha! And us? Could it be that these parched plains will become our safe haven in this deployment until next spring, could it be that we bought equipment and took heroic selfies against the background of the neglected summer camp below Frunze in Kherson in vain?

Then there was that month and in a semi-conscious state at our training camp with frightening and disturbing rumors about being sent to Bessarabia – as if we were some kind of embarrassment that they were trying to hide from the Americans, who were providing training at the camp, as if we were incapable of protecting the eastern borders. "ATO, you've got to be kidding me, this is a job for special forces, someone with a properly intense gaze depicted in advertising billboards." And then this disturbing word "deployment." Tomorrow, we're leaving already. For how long? Well, for at least a month for sure. Everything there will depend on your fighting spirit, your fighting skills, and on the situation on the front.

I don't know what fighting spirit is left, but our military skills and the situation at the front have extended our stay here to ten months.

The gentle autumn changed to a wet and cold winter. Then there was spring: rainy and light as expected, and finally summer. Quiet and windless. Hot air, beetles, flies, the scent of clay. The sun evaporating body moisture, a dry dust rising from the least breath of wind, the sharp blades of the high grass cutting into sticky skin, the bed bugs hiding in clothes and in sleeping bags. Worn out from the heat, soldiers wandered at their posts waiting for orders to release them from their fifth tour of mobilization. In conversations we often spoke of past events: the vendors from a small city in Kherson, feats of love, our morbid desire to serve and be useful, our salary of two thousand hryvnias, our mobilization for our third or even fourth tour of duty, our worry free nomadic life on the Black Sea coast. And we shared plans for life after demobilization.

What changed from then? What images and evils were left? What did we accomplish? What will we go home with, what will we tell our children, and what will we only tell close friends?

Broken families, unpaid credit, unfinished renovations, hoarse voices, dark tans, blackened eyes with orange capillaries, washed-out shirts? and T-shirts white from salt. Someone's son was born, someone's father died, someone didn't make it back, leaving both son and father behind. This is fate of the fifth tour of mobilization. Welcome home.

The Apricots of Donbas

You can't amaze me with apricots. I was born and raised in the Cherkasy region, which is full of apricots. I spent my entire childhood squashing mushy orange carpets under my feet and bicycle tires. I spent three whole weeks in July almost exclusively eating apricots, being able to distinguish the different kinds by their taste: from the early "Alyosha" to the sweet "Nikita" or the larger "Ananasnyi." The apricots grew by my house, beyond my house, and along the street. They grew in my grandmother's yard and my uncle's yard, they grew in the alleyways where my grandma and grandpa lived. They grew along both sides of the road, by the stadium, and by the Dnipro River, instead of willows. They surrounded factories and businesses. All of my childhood I have lived among black knotty apricot trees. White blossoms, yellow fruit – it was beautiful. It was a Mediterranean-like environment. A blessing, a gift. Driving into the city you saw endless trees filled with ripe hanging fruit. The whole city was like an orchard providing nourishment to the children and old people who were the ones most fond of apricots. And then when I moved to Kyiv and I only saw apricots at street markets and supermarkets. And in Cherkasy the old trees are dying off now and new ones weren't planted. After the Chernobyl catastrophe, they stopped planting fruit trees. People believed that any fruit would be contaminated by radioactive dust.

Here on the fields of Luhansk, there are no apricots. None at all. There aren't even any fir or pine trees. Only oaks and acacias. But if you just travel to the closest populated area, you will see your first apricots. I spent all of April at my post, not venturing out anywhere else, so this year I missed out on seeing the white flowers with brown centers. I didn't have the time, or, frankly, the desire. There was a war and we were its soldiers. The long winter ended with new travails. But then suddenly it was July, as dry and hot as a Donbas summer should be. The inevitable prospect of demobilization revived our strength and energy – we dared to start making plans, sketching out strategies for our future lives, and started going into the city more often. We had the audacity to call a taxi right up to our checkpoint, in order to bypass headquarters and all existing checkpoints. For 150 the taxi driver dropped us off in Popasna, where we sat in a coffee shop for hours, eating chicken *kotlety*, salads, and ice-cream.

Now is the time for apricots. Like the ones from my childhood, when the city literally changed color from gray and black to green and orange. Apricots are everywhere. It seems that they grow amid demolished buildings, in potholes on the roads, from windows, blown out by explosive shock waves. There are so many of them, and in the city there is so much sun that it's hard to believe, that a kilometer from here are positions, which are pounded all day and night by mortar and rocket launchers. Life goes on in the city. At first glance, it doesn't appear to be like one located close to the front line, instead it seems like a typical provincial town: a tired dog naps in the dust near the post office, taxi drivers drink kvass in the shade of some chestnuts and linden trees, young mothers with strollers walk along the park, some teenage boys race around on bicycles. Only the sand bags near the commander's office and the military vehicles parked along both sides of the road give away the proximity of the war. And so we, having purchased apricots at the grocery store (yes, yes, at the store, because it was unseemly for us fine, demobilized soldiers to climb trees), we returned to our trenches and dugouts. Only an hour ago, tired out from food and sweet drinks, we were strolling through the city in washed uniforms and polished boots, and now, having already changed into shorts and torn T-shirts, we are staring past our encampment to where a suspicious-looking smoke is rising.

Remembering "apricots put on their helmets," from *The Apricots of Donbas*, a poetry collection by Lyuba Yakimchuk, I eat the sweet fruit from Moldova. I feel how that all this will soon end for me and wonder how long I would remember it all. Quiet trees, loud explosions, long talks, tart kvass, painful sunburns, new relationships and old habits, sleepless nights, familiar voices on the phone, a lush green field before us, the foul odor from the trench, total emptiness somewhere deep inside me, cautious dreams of a peaceful life, the boundless sky of Luhansk, and warm apricots. It doesn't matter that they are from somewhere where war exists only on television and computer monitors.

The Last Night

They let Vlad go three days early, so only Sanya and I were left.

For a parting gift, Vlad gets us a bottle of wine. I accompany him to head-quarters. We embrace, we cry. He drives away and I go back to the outpost with a bottle of dry red wine and half a kilo of wieners. That evening Sanya and I sit by the fire and talk a lot. We get drunk from the wine, as if it was vodka. Having had our fill of the wieners, we sit poking at the coals with skewers and think about everything that has happened in the last fourteen months. Later, already in our bunker, lying in our sleeping bags, we spend a long time sharing secrets and revelations. It seemed that if we didn't do it now, we never would.

I thank him for teaching me how to be a man, how not to be afraid, and for teaching me to say what I honestly think. He also thanks me. He thanks me for not letting him down, even though he wasn't sure of me at first. He says that he didn't trust me, that he was afraid that in a difficult situation I would get scared and, so, get us in trouble.

That last night, Sanya asks me to read my stories to him. I read one, another one, and he asks for more, saying it is better than watching a mov-ie. I am surprised, because I know how tiring it can be to listen to prose. But he insists, and I read. It's already one in the morning and we have to get up at seven to get ready for the road, say goodbye to everyone, shake hands, hold back tears, smoke outside on the path, but we talk and talk, as if we hadn't talked enough during our thirteen months together. And we don't want to sleep, and we don't want to make the journey, we only want to get out of here quickly and forget everything, but we also want to remember everything forever. And we wonder how to make sense of it all, wonder how can we live with all we've experienced, and how we can live leaving all this behind?

We get up at six. We wash, we brush our teeth, we put on freshly washed clothes. We walk between the bunkers, we say goodbye to those who are staying behind, for a week, for two, or until the end of their individual service period. I want to say something meaningful, but end up saying nothing instead. I want to bestow heaps of good wishes and promises, but deliver only trite expressions and chat on familiar topics. We depart for headquarters. Of course, with the same driver we've had for many months in our old car, swallowing dust. We drive past our outposts, finally wait at headquarters for our documents, talk again, grow silent again. Officers from other platoons come up and thank us for our service. Soldiers approach and solemnly shake our hands.

The heat is oppressive. Khan, the scouting unit's German shepherd kicks up dust, dragging a kitten between his teeth, tries to play with it, but the kitten is frightened by the scary ordeal. Roman, the electrician from the sniper unit, walks up. A month ago, he was transferred to our military prison in Platoon 1 for some transgressions. He holds some cables in his hands and sighs audibly. He says that he'll leave with the last of our bunch. Our sergeant, Ivanych, who ably served with us during our entire time at the outpost, is noticeably worried – he doesn't want us to leave. But we cheer him up.

"Ivanych, don't be frightened, you'll be leaving soon anyway. In December," we add and laugh.

We hear rounds of machine gun fire coming from the nearest fighting position. But this doesn't concern us anymore. We wait for them to finally give us our military tickets and discharge papers, for the command to get on the bus, salute us and release us to drift on, but in a different direction. One warmer and not as turbulent.

Sanya! My friend Sanya! We still have forty minutes together and then you will arrive in Artemivska and journey to your mining town to drink cold beer and bathe your tired body in the Samar river. Then I will travel seven hundred kilometers more in the snow-white Intercity train car, drinking away my boredom with a tonic or cold cola. We will say goodbye, but we'll certainly meet again. Those like me always meet those like you again. Even if this will be not in a subway or between the gates at the Munich airport.

Uncle Lyosha is traveling with us. He has two weeks until his demobilization. He is going to Vinnytsya, to the hospital. After saying goodbye to Sanya, we are left together, two neighbors. In Kostiantynivka, while waiting for the train, we stand in the shade and smoke, talk about the future, and about beer. I recall how on training exercises in Shyrlan, when they left us on the steppe for three days without water and cigarettes, we walked together to a village, that was occupied exclusively by Tatars and Roma, and where we happened on a store where we each bought a bottle of cold beer from Mykolaiv. Exhausted from thirst and upset with our commanders, we just sat down near the store on the curb and greedily guzzled down the cold beer. I remind the old man about this episode and he laughs, but something close to a curse escapes from his lips. There are still thirty minutes left until the train comes. We look at the crowd that is made up of mainly young people who are being seated in the minibuses: Kostiantynivka – Donetsk, Koctiantynivka – Horlivka, Kostiantynivka – Snizhne.

I am silent. But Uncle Lyosha isn't silent: *This is life! Back and forth, back and forth, you yellow-toothed bastards!*

P.S.

It was in my youth that I first decided to write a book about war. War not in the usual sense, but the one, which existed in the mind of my protagonist, a person who really played one of the defining and most significant roles in my becoming an adult, defining my worldview and outlook, broadening my understanding, and enabling me to become the person that I am.

This book was supposed to be a unique biography of a former special forces officer and a military spy, an officer who walked over many lands in his Soviet army boots – from the Czech Republic to Nicaragua and Afghanistan, and then ended up in a three bedroom on the outskirts of Cherkasy. He was called Pylyp Petrovych. He was born in 1947, and in childhood he had the nickname Kaltenbrunner, due to his tall stature and his father's rank as a colonel in the KGB. Later he served as a paratrooper, attended military school, participated in military operations in different corners of the world, spent eight years in Afghanistan, and served in counterintelligence. Finally, there were wounds and concussions.

He moved into our apartment, obviously counting on becoming a member of our family, surrounding himself with the glow of family comfort, love, cleanliness, harmony and the right to well-deserved rest. An international warrior, a hero, lieutenant colonel, paratrooper, scout, a good father and a tender lover, endlessly witty and always generous. My grandmother also counted on the fact that we would gladly acknowledge her right to happiness. But Pylyp, as it turned out, drank like a fish. He drank cognac, wine, vodka, beer, liqueurs, port wine, homemade drinks, apple spirits. He drank hawthorn tinctures, colognes, extracts and also denatured alcohol. This whole process was accompanied by psychotic episodes, constant fear, attempts at domestic violence, and delusions. Drunk, he sharply reacted to any loud noises or the sudden appearance of a person in his range of vision. His triggers were the sounds of rain, music, a child's cry outside, or any appearance of weapons. Then he would roll his eyes, bare his teeth and growl. This growling could only end in violence. Usually Pylyp punched the wall or door. Rarely, although it did happen, he went after my grandmother. My grandmother never let anyone lift a hand to her, so for safety she kept a wooden barrel full of sticks in reserve with which she pacified her cohabitant. When sober, Pylyp didn't even allow himself to swear. He acted like a well-behaved, educated, decent and tactful person. His grandmother was a countess, her maiden name was Pototska, and she was the direct descendent of Stanislav Shensny, so Pylyp was able to get a decent aristocratic education. He ate with a fork and knife, kept handkerchiefs in his pocket, and knew the intricacies of etiquette. It is the true that that was the etiquette of the apparatchik milieu, very unsophisticated, but that's beside the point... He taught me how to hit a head properly, how to break a nose with my palm, and he played chess and basketball with me. Then when drunk again, he drove my whole family to the edge of their tolerance, ruthlessly damaged our relationship, ignored decency, and caused us to have zero regard for military people in general and Afghans in particular.

He lived in our apartment for all of the nineties and for a year after. I was always drawn to him, like to anything forbidden, like the dirty cliques in my neighborhood, to drugs, and porn. Of course, they were unable to teach me anything wise, good, or of eternal use, however, they completely gave me that invaluable experience that turns a boy into a man. Throughout our close existence in those 40 square meters, Pylyp was a forbidden phenomenon to me. At some juncture my mother forbid me from inter-acting with him, from talking, greeting, and noticing him. For her he was a hopeless person, destructive, lost. For her he existed only as an oppressive phantom that came to torture her and to fill her life with grief and complete depression. For me he was a person, who could teach me those important lessons that a father could teach a son: to survive, to fight, to love, to cry, to survive disillusionment and despair, and to temper expressions of delight at triumphs and victories, and above all to love life…and always remember death.

When he left, I think, at the end of 2001, I thought about writing a book about him. Really, he was a deserving candidate for a protagonist, whose course in life was questionable, generated sadness, and had a place for heroism. The war that remained with him became mine. Empathy, child-hood vulnerability, and good memory allowed me to absorb many of his memories of severed heads in military vehicles blown up by the land mines and tortured Soviet generals in the damp basements of counterintelligence. From Pylyp's descriptive and expansive visions of war I selected some threads of narrative and used them to form my own stories. Sometimes it seemed to me that I knew more about the Soviet intervention than Pylyp knew, from there came my idea for the book (Lord, I thought about this seriously already at 15!) which continued to grow. However, time passed, and I didn't write one sentence about Pylyp or the war. Moreover, I didn't think about him for months. And if I remembered certain occurrences from the past, they were mostly memories of comical events.

I saw him for the last time during the Orange Revolution. By then he was a complete drunk, he hung out near the Central Market, for a bottle he moved baskets of vegetables. He didn't wash his clothes, shaved once a week, and often slept in that very market among the tents. Is he still alive? I don't know…

And so now, with my own war in my head, with my own experiences in this filthy trench epic where I clearly saw the "game of war," I understood Pylyp in a way that I didn't understand him before. He became closer – as if I had the chance to crawl into his head and see his war, to accept it and in some measure like it.

For that reason I again felt the inescapable desire to write this book about it.

Rivne – Partisans – Frunze – Popasna – Mykolayiv – Kyiv, 2015-2016

Ravens before Noah

by Susanna Harutyunyan

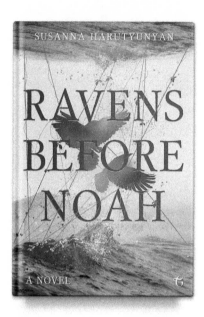

This novel is set in the Armenian mountains sometime in 1915-1960. An old man and a new born baby boy escape from the Hamidian massacres in Turkey in 1894 and hide themselves in the ruins of a demolished and abandoned village. The village soon becomes a shelter for many others, who flee from problems with the law, their families, or their past lives. The villagers survive in this secret shelter, cut off from the rest of the world, by selling or bartering their agricultural products in the villages beneath the mountain.

Years pass by, and the child saved by the old man grows into a young man, Harout. He falls for a beautiful girl who arrived in the village after being tortured by Turkish soldiers. She is pregnant and the old women of the village want to kill the twin baby girls as soon as they are born, to wash away the shame…

Buy it > www.glagoslav.com

The Flying Dutchman

by Anatoly Kudryavitsky

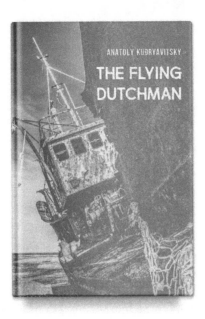

Some time in the 1970s, Konstantin Alpheyev, a well-known Russian musicologist, finds himself in trouble with the KGB, the Russian secret police, after the death of his girlfriend, for which one of their officers may have been responsible. He has to flee from the city and to go into hiding. He rents an old house located on the bank of a big Russian river, and lives there like a recluse observing nature and working on his new book about Wagner. The house, a part of an old barge, undergoes strange metamorphoses rebuilding itself as a medieval schooner, and Alpheyev begins to identify himself with the Flying Dutchman. Meanwhile, the police locate his new whereabouts and put him under surveillance. A chain of strange events in the nearby village makes the police officer contact the KGB, and the latter figure out who the new tenant of the old house actually is.

Buy it > www.glagoslav.com

Mikhail Bulgakov: The Life and Times

by Marietta Chudakova

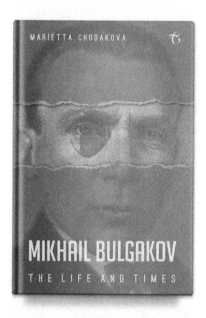

Marietta Chudakova's biography of Bulgakov was first published in 1988 and remains the most authoritative and comprehensive study of the writer's life ever produced. It has received acclaim for the journalistic style in which it is written: the author draws on unpublished manuscripts and early drafts of Bulgakov's novels to bring the writer to life. She also explores archive documents and memoirs written by some of Bulgakov's contemporaries so as to construct a comprehensive and nuanced portrait of the writer and his life and times. The scholar casts light on Bulgakov's life with an unrivalled eye for detail and a huge amount of affection for the writer and his works.

Mikhail Bulgakov: The Life and Times will be of particular interest to international researchers studying Mikhail Bulgakov's life and works, and is recommended to a broader audience worldwide.

Buy it > www.glagoslav.com

Glagoslav Publications Catalogue

- *The Time of Women* by Elena Chizhova
- *Andrei Tarkovsky: The Collector of Dreams* by Layla Alexander-Garrett
- *Andrei Tarkovsky - A Life on the Cross* by Lyudmila Boyadzhieva
- *Sin* by Zakhar Prilepin
- *Hardly Ever Otherwise* by Maria Matios
- *Khatyn* by Ales Adamovich
- *The Lost Button* by Irene Rozdobudko
- *Christened with Crosses* by Eduard Kochergin
- *The Vital Needs of the Dead* by Igor Sakhnovsky
- *The Sarabande of Sara's Band* by Larysa Denysenko
- *A Poet and Bin Laden* by Hamid Ismailov
- *Watching The Russians (Dutch Edition)* by Maria Konyukova
- *Kobzar* by Taras Shevchenko
- *The Stone Bridge* by Alexander Terekhov
- *Moryak* by Lee Mandel
- *King Stakh's Wild Hunt* by Uladzimir Karatkevich
- *The Hawks of Peace* by Dmitry Rogozin
- *Harlequin's Costume* by Leonid Yuzefovich
- *Depeche Mode* by Serhii Zhadan
- *The Grand Slam and other stories (Dutch Edition)* by Leonid Andreev
- *METRO 2033 (Dutch Edition)* by Dmitry Glukhovsky
- *METRO 2034 (Dutch Edition)* by Dmitry Glukhovsky
- *A Russian Story* by Eugenia Kononenko
- *Herstories, An Anthology of New Ukrainian Women Prose Writers*
- *The Battle of the Sexes Russian Style* by Nadezhda Ptushkina
- *A Book Without Photographs* by Sergey Shargunov
- *Down Among The Fishes* by Natalka Babina
- *disUNITY* by Anatoly Kudryavitsky
- *Sankya* by Zakhar Prilepin
- *Wolf Messing* by Tatiana Lungin
- *Good Stalin* by Victor Erofeyev
- *Solar Plexus* by Rustam Ibragimbekov
- *Don't Call me a Victim!* by Dina Yafasova
- *Poetin (Dutch Edition)* by Chris Hutchins and Alexander Korobko

- *Forefathers' Eve* by Adam Mickiewicz
- *One-Two* by Igor Eliseev
- *Girls, be Good* by Bojan Babić
- *Time of the Octopus* by Anatoly Kucherena
- *The Grand Harmony* by Bohdan Ihor Antonych
- *The Selected Lyric Poetry Of Maksym Rylsky*
- *The Shining Light* by Galymkair Mutanov
- *The Frontier: 28 Contemporary Ukrainian Poets - An Anthology*
- *Acropolis: The Wawel Plays* by Stanisław Wyspiański
- *Contours of the City* by Attyla Mohylny
- *Conversations Before Silence: The Selected Poetry of Oles Ilchenko*
- *The Secret History of my Sojourn in Russia* by Jaroslav Hašek
- *Mirror Sand: An Anthology of Russian Short Poems in English Translation* (A Bilingual Edition)
- *Maybe We're Leaving* by Jan Balaban
- *Death of the Snake Catcher* by Ak Welsapar
- *A Brown Man in Russia: Perambulations Through A Siberian Winter* by Vijay Menon
- *Hard Times* by Ostap Vyshnia
- *The Flying Dutchman* by Anatoly Kudryavitsky
- *Nikolai Gumilev's Africa* by Nikolai Gumilev
- *Combustions* by Srđan Srdić
- *The Sonnets* by Adam Mickiewicz
- *Dramatic Works* by Zygmunt Krasiński
- *Four Plays* by Juliusz Słowacki
- *Little Zinnobers* by Elena Chizhova
- *We Are Building Capitalism! Moscow in Transition 1992-1997*
- *The Nuremberg Trials* by Alexander Zvyagintsev
- *The Hemingway Game* by Evgeni Grishkovets
- *A Flame Out at Sea* by Dmitry Novikov
- *Jesus' Cat* by Grig
- *Want a Baby and Other Plays* by Sergei Tretyakov
- *I Mikhail Bulgakov: The Life and Times* by Marietta Chudakova
- *Leonardo's Handwriting* by Dina Rubina
- *A Burglar of the Better Sort* by Tytus Czyżewski
- *The Mouseiad and other Mock Epics* by Ignacy Krasicki
- *Ravens before Noah* by Susanna Harutyunyan
- *Duel* by Borys Antonenko-Davydovych
- *An English Queen and Stalingrad* by Natalia Kulishenko
- *Point Zero* by Narek Malian
  More coming soon...

CPSIA information can be obtained
at www.ICGtesting.com
Printed in the USA
LVHW091711200322
713906LV00002B/35